# Crown of the Mist

Zora Stone

Print ISBN: 978-1-971405-04-9

Publisher: Smut by Design

www.zorastone.com

*For the ones who have spent too long seeing themselves through shattered glass—may you one day recognize the beauty in every broken piece.*

# Trigger Warnings

Thank you for reading *Crown of the Mist*! This book contains themes and content that may be triggering to some readers. Please review the following warnings before proceeding:

**Major Content Warnings:**

**Emotional and Psychological Themes**

- **Childhood Abuse & Neglect** – References to Bree's abusive father and neglectful upbringing.

- **Domestic Violence** – Mentions of past physical and emotional abuse.

- **Gaslighting & Manipulation** – Instances of psychological control and coercion.

- **PTSD & Trauma Responses** – Flashbacks, dissociation, panic attacks, and difficulty with touch.

- **Depression & Suicidal Ideation** – Themes of self-worth struggles, isolation, and intrusive thoughts.

- **Self-Harm Scars & Body Image Issues** – Mentions of scars from past abuse and Bree's struggles with self-image.

## Violence, Death & Harassment

- **Sexual Assault/Harassment** – Includes a scene where Bree is threatened and touched against her will by her landlord; references to past sexual violence.

- **Stalking & Surveillance** – Hidden cameras in Bree's apartment; her landlord and father monitoring her.

- **Violence & Threats** – Physical confrontations, implied past violence, and threats against Bree and others.

- **Death & Loss** – The death of a close elderly figure (Mrs. Henderson), grief and processing loss.

- **Mild Torture/Implied Imprisonment** – References to past or off-screen situations where characters were held against their will.

## Substance Use & Power Imbalances

- **Substance Abuse** – A character (Phil) is frequently intoxicated and uses alcohol as a means of control.

- **Forced Proximity & Power Imbalance** – Bree is forced into uncomfortable situations due to financial and social constraints.

## Paranormal & Supernatural Themes

- **Paranormal/Magical Influence** – Themes of supernatural forces influencing thoughts, behaviors, and reality.

This list is provided to ensure a safe reading experience. If any of these topics are personally distressing, please read with care.

Thank you for your support and for stepping into Bree's journey.

*— Zora Stone*

# CONTENTS

# Chapter 1
## BREE

I trudge down the cracked sidewalk, my feet aching in my worn-out sneakers. The late afternoon sun casts long shadows that make the rundown buildings loom like disapproving giants. Every breath brings a mix of exhaust fumes, rotting garbage, and the sickly-sweet scent of the flowering weeds pushing through the concrete.

*Just another glamorous day in paradise.*

My skin prickles before I hear them. The car engine slows, and then—

"Hey, sweetheart! Why don't you smile for me?"

I keep my eyes fixed on the ground, counting cracks in the sidewalk. *One, two, three.* My hands curl into fists inside my pockets, nails biting into my palms. *Four, five, six.*

"C'mon, baby, don't be like that!"

Their laughter follows me around the corner, sticky and unwanted like everything else today. I resist the urge to look over my shoulder, to check if they're following.

*Almost home. Just a few more blocks.*

As I walk, my mind drifts back to my shift at Maple Grove. Mrs. Henderson's arthritis was acting up again, her gnarled fingers trembling as she tried to hold her fork. I'd helped her eat, pretending not to notice the tears of frustration in her eyes. Then Mr. Jacobs had another episode. I'd spent half the morning coaxing him back to reality, reminding him where he was, who I was. "You look just like my Sarah," he'd said, patting my hand. "She always took such good care of me." The weariness settles deep in my bones, a familiar ache that never quite goes away.

I fish my keys out of my bag as I approach my building. The Ridgeview Apartments—or as I like to call it, The Shoe Box. It's not much, but it's mine. Sort of. As long as I can keep scraping together rent each month.

I'm still digging for my keys when I feel it—that prickle on the back of my neck that makes my stomach clench. I glance up, and there he is. Phil, my illustrious landlord, leaning against his doorway about twenty feet away. His bloodshot eyes creep over me like insects, making my skin crawl. The sharp, sour stench of alcohol reaches me before his words do. An open beer bottle dangles from his meaty fingers—probably not his first, definitely not his last. His shirt is rumpled and stained, stretched tight across his gut like plastic wrap over spoiled meat. A leer spreads across his face as our eyes meet, and I have to suppress a shudder.

*Great. Just what I need to cap off this stellar day.*

"Evening, Bree," he slurs, lifting his bottle in a mock salute. "Looking good, as always."

I grit my teeth, willing my hands not to shake as I finally close my fingers around my keys. "Hi, Phil," I mutter, not bothering to hide the ice in my voice.

He pushes off from the doorframe, swaying slightly as he takes a step toward me. "How about you and me have a little chat about this month's rent?" His grin widens, revealing yellowed teeth. "I'm sure we could work something out."

My stomach turns. I know exactly what kind of "arrangement" he's hinting at. The same one he's been pushing since I moved in.

"I'll have it by Friday," I say, fumbling with my keys. "Just like we agreed."

Phil chuckles, a low, unpleasant sound. "Come on now, don't be like that. I'm trying to help you out here." He takes another step closer, and I can see the sheen of sweat on his forehead. "Pretty girl like you shouldn't have to worry about money."

I back away, my heart pounding. "I said I'll have it Friday."

The lock sticks, as usual. I jiggle the key, muttering under my breath until it finally gives. "Night," I yell at Phil without looking back as the door creaks open, and I step into the musty silence of my studio. Home sweet home.

I kick off my shoes and collapse onto the sagging couch, staring up at the water-stained ceiling. Another night alone stretches out before me. No texts, no calls. The guys are probably hanging out at home, laughing, sharing beers. Maybe one of them found a nice girl. A familiar ache blooms in my chest, but I push it away. It's better this way. They don't need me holding them back. That's really all I've done for them over the last eighteen years. And really, they're better off without me. They all deserve to find someone to love, who makes them happy and makes them better. I know that kind of thing exists. Probably.

*Just not for me.*

I roll onto my side, curling into myself. The silence presses in, broken only by the hum of the ancient refrigerator and the muffled sounds of my neighbors arguing through the paper-thin walls. This is fine. This is what

I wanted, right? No complications, no one to disappoint. No one to hurt me again.

I close my eyes, trying to ignore the whisper in the back of my mind. The one that sounds suspiciously like longing. Like regret.

A faint shimmer catches my attention, and I open my eyes to see tendrils of mist curling at the edges of my vision. My breath catches. Not now. Please, not now. I'm too tired for this.

The mist lingers at the edges of the room, silent and watching, like a presence waiting to be acknowledged. It's always there in moments like this, when I'm alone with my thoughts. Watching. Waiting. For what, I've never known.

"Just go away," I whisper.

It lingers for a moment longer, then dissipates into nothing, leaving me alone with the silence and my thoughts.

I bury my face in my hands, willing the events of the day, the guys, to calm in my mind. I'm failing spectacularly when a knock at the door makes me jump.

"Bree?" Rhett's voice cuts through the haze like a lifeline I'm not sure I deserve. "You in there?"

I squeeze my eyes shut, debating whether to answer. Silence is safer. Silence means no one gets too close. Maybe if I wait long enough, he'll leave—like everyone else always does.

"Bree." Lower this time, but with that edge of steel that makes my stomach flip. "I know you're there. Open up."

When I pull open the door, he fills the frame like he always has, steady and solid and so frustratingly present. His sharp green eyes scan my face, and something in his expression softens just enough to make my chest ache. I step out quickly, pulling the door shut behind me before he can peek inside. He's never been in my apartment, none of them have. Some walls need to stay up.

His presence fills the narrow hallway, and I press myself against the doorframe, trying to maintain distance even as part of me aches to lean into his warmth. The familiar scent of cedar and smoke wraps around me, making my chest tight with longing.

You okay?" he asks, his voice low.

"Peachy," I mutter, leaning against the doorframe.

He raises an eyebrow. "You look like hell."

"Thanks for the boost of confidence," I snap, though there's no heat behind it.

Rhett exhales and rubs the back of his neck. "Look, I'm not here to argue. I just...wanted to check on you. You didn't answer my texts."

I glance away, guilt twisting in my stomach. "I've been busy."

"Too busy to let me know you're alive?"

"It's not like that."

"Then what is it like?" he asks, his voice soft but insistent. "Because from where I'm standing, it looks a hell of a lot like you're trying to push us all away."

My throat tightens, but I don't have an answer for him. Not one I can say out loud, anyway.

At my silence he just sighs and steps closer, his hand brushing my shoulder. "You don't have to do this alone, Bree," he says quietly. "You never did."

The weight of his words presses down on me, and for a moment, I want to believe him. But I know better.

"I'm fine," I whisper, stepping back into the safety of my apartment. "Really."

Rhett watches me for a long moment, his jaw tightening before he nods. "Sure. Fine."

He turns and walks away, his footsteps echoing down the hall like a countdown I can't stop. Each step drives home how good I am at this—pushing people away, staying safely broken.

I click the door shut and slide down against it, the worn wood rough against my back through my thin shirt. My forehead drops to my knees as I try to breathe through the tightness in my chest. The mist curls around me, its cool tendrils brushing against my skin like a concerned touch I don't deserve. It weaves between my fingers where they grip my legs, persistent and present in a way that makes my throat burn.

"Stop," I whisper, but I'm not sure if I'm talking to the mist or myself. Maybe both. The silence of my apartment presses in, broken only by the steady drip of the leaky faucet and the sound of my ragged breathing.

Something warm slides down my cheek—a tear I didn't give permission to fall. I swipe it away roughly, but more follow, silent betrayals that prove how weak I really am.

# Chapter 2
## BREE

*The smell of burnt toast and cigarettes fills the apartment. I sit cross-legged on my bed, clutching my stuffed bear, its fur matted from too many nights of soaking up tears. I press my face into its soft belly, trying to block out the yelling from the next room, but every word cuts through the thin walls like knives.*

*"You're just going to leave?!" Dad's voice makes my stomach twist into knots. "After everything I've done for you?"*

*"I can't do this anymore, Kevin." Mom's voice wavers between sharp and broken. "I've tried. God, I've tried. But I'm done."*

*I press my hands over my ears, squeezing my eyes shut until colors burst behind my lids. Their voices seep through anyway, poison through cracks.*

*"You're not thinking about Bree." Dad's voice turns mean, the way it does right before things break. "What kind of mother just walks out on her kid?"*

*"Everything I do is for her!" Mom's voice cracks like glass, something wild and desperate in it that I've never heard before. "You don't understand. You never did."*

*That makes my heart stutter. My fingers dig into the bear's fur until I feel threads pop. Mom wouldn't leave me. She wouldn't.*

*"You think this is easy for me?" Her voice drops, heavy with something that sounds like grief. "I can't stay here, Kevin. I just can't."*

*I climb off the bed and tiptoe toward the door, my socks silent on the worn carpet. The crack of light from the hallway cuts across my room, just enough to see the tear in my bear's ear. I fixate on it, blinking hard against the sting in my eyes.*

*The front door slams, shaking the walls. Then everything goes quiet.*

*"Mom?" I whisper, my voice trembling. My legs feel heavy as I inch toward the hallway. "Mommy?"*

*Dad's voice explodes again, cutting through the stillness. "Damn it, Claire!" He throws something—I don't know what—and the crash makes me jump. "You're gonna regret this!"*

*I run to my window, pressing my hands against the cold glass. Mom's figure cuts through the darkness below, moving so fast she's almost running. Her long dark hair streams behind her like a flag of surrender.*

*"Mom!" I bang on the window, but she doesn't look back. "Mom, please!"*

*She reaches the corner where the streetlight flickers, that broken one that never seems to work right.*

*For a second, she pauses.*

*And I think—I hope—she's going to turn around.*

*But then...*

*A faint glow halos her figure—soft, almost like moonlight—just for a breath of a second.*

*I blink.*

*And she steps into the shadows.*

*The night swallows her whole.*

*One moment she's there, and the next... nothing.*

*Empty sidewalk. Yellow lamplight.*

*I shrink back from the window, clutching the bear to my chest, and slide to the floor. My knees hit the carpet as the first sob breaks free, and I cry into its fur until my chest hurts.*

I wake with a start, gasping for air like I've just surfaced from deep water. My chest feels heavy, and the ghost of my mother's retreating figure lingers behind my eyes. The apartment is silent, but it doesn't feel empty. The mist is here, just like it always is after these nightmares. These memories.

It clings to the floor, faint and formless, lingering at the edges of my vision. I sit up, rubbing my face, and glance at the corner where it's gathered. "Not now," I mutter. It doesn't move, just hovers there like a silent observer.

My hand reaches for the journal on the coffee table, the one I've been writing in since I was a kid. I flip to a blank page and start scribbling, the words spilling out before I can stop them.

*It was the same dream. The same memory. That night replaying over and over like a broken record I can't throw away. The way she just... disappeared. Sometimes I wonder if I imagined that part. If my child's mind made up the impossible because the truth was too hard to handle.*

The pen hovers over the page, the words blurring together. *Why did she leave? Was it really for me like she claimed? Did I do something wrong?* I slam the journal shut before I can write anything else.

The sharp ring of my phone makes me jump. I grab it off the table, my stomach twisting when I see Gray's name on the screen. For a second, I consider ignoring it, but I know better. He's not the type to let it go.

"Hey," I say, trying to sound normal.

"Bree." Gray's voice is calm, steady, but I can hear the edge of worry in it. "You free this morning?"

"I have a shift later."

"Then you've got time for coffee," he says, like it's already decided. "Theo's coming too."

"I—"

"No excuses." His voice softens, but there's steel underneath it. "Just meet us. Mercer's. One hour."

The line goes dead before I can argue.

*Fuck.*

I drag myself off the couch, my feet hitting the cold floor. The mist hovers at the edges of my vision, but I ignore it. I've gotten good at that.

The bathroom is dark when I step inside, cool air curling around me as I shut the door. I flip the switch, and the overhead light hums to life, flickering weakly, hesitating—before finally settling into a dim, sickly glow. The old fluorescent bulb casts uneven shadows against the peeling paint, making my reflection in the mirror look even worse than I feel.

I don't need a second opinion. I already know I look like hell.

Dark circles stand out against my pale skin, making the scattered freckles across my nose more pronounced. My wavy brown hair is a tangled mess, falling in limp strands past my shoulders. I reach up to push it back, but my fingers snag in a knot, reminding me just how long it's been since I cared enough to do more than throw it in a bun. I look like I feel. Awesome.

I lean closer, studying my reflection with a grimace. Mom's eyes stare back at me, light green with flecks of gold - the only part of myself I don't mind looking at. Everything else feels wrong somehow. Too soft, too curvy, too much. My full lips, my wider hips, the chest that makes me want to hide under baggy hoodies - all of it feeling like an invitation for the wrong kind of attention. I step back, pulling my oversized sleep shirt tighter around myself.

I turn on the shower, wincing at the loud groan of the pipes. The water sputters, then steadies into a weak stream. It's lukewarm at best, but it's better than nothing. I step into the cramped stall, ducking my head to avoid the low showerhead.

As I soap up my body, I keep my eyes fixed on the cracked tile of the shower wall. I can't bear to look down, to see the map of pain etched across my skin. My fingers trace over the raised scar on my shoulder, a souvenir from the time Dad threw a bottle at me when I was thirteen. I shudder, remembering the sting of glass and the metallic scent of blood mixing with cheap whiskey.

There's another scar, jagged and ugly, running along my hip. That one's from Jason, my first real boyfriend.

My first real boyfriend at 21.

Pathetic.

Most people had already been through breakups, makeups, and whirlwind love stories by then. **Meanwhile, I spent my early twenties dodging questions about why I'd never had one.** It wasn't like I wasn't interested—I just... never let anyone close enough.

Then Jason came along, all charm and effortless attention, making me believe I was finally **normal.** That I could have what everyone else did.

He seemed so sweet at first, always bringing me flowers and telling me how beautiful I was. Until the night he got drunk and decided I'd been flirting with the bartender.

I'd never seen someone's eyes go so cold so fast.

And I haven't really had one since.

Not really. Not in any way that mattered. Not when the thought of hands on my skin still makes my stomach twist.

I scrub harder, as if I could wash away the memories along with the grime. My hand skims over my ribs, feeling the slight bump where one never quite healed right after Dad kicked me down the stairs. I was sixteen then, and it was the night I found a single daisy on my windowsill.

The first of many, though I never figured out who left them.

A ghost of a smile touches my lips—it's the reason daisies are my favorite flower.

The smile fades as quickly as it came.

If they ever saw the scars, what would they think? Would they piece together the story written across my skin? Would they see the truth I try so hard to hide?

Would they finally understand how weak I really am?

It doesn't matter. I'll never let them see. Never.

I sigh, realizing if I don't stop scrubbing soon I won't have any skin left. Turning off the shower means wrestling with the rusty handle until the weak stream finally stops. The mirror has fogged over, giving me a brief reprieve from my reflection, but as I towel off, the steam starts to clear. Shadows under my eyes come into focus, stark against my flushed skin. I run a hand through my damp hair, letting out a bitter laugh. "You look great, Bree. A real catch."

My closet is nearly empty - another reminder of all the things I can't afford to replace. The familiar softness of my old hoodie welcomes me as I pull it on. Armor against the world, against their concern, against everything I don't want to face.

The mist swirls around my feet as I grab my keys and phone, almost expectant. "Not today," I mutter, stepping over it and into the hallway. But today isn't going to give me a choice.

# Chapter 3
## BREE

Each step toward Mercer's feels heavier than the last. My mind races with excuses to turn back, but I know Gray. He'd probably show up at my door if I bailed, and that would be worse. Having him there, in my space, seeing how I really live.

The café buzzes with morning conversation and clinking mugs as I push through the door. I tug my hoodie closer, scanning the room. I could still leave. Turn around now and avoid the inevitable questions, the concerned looks that make me feel like I'm drowning.

Gray catches my eye from the corner table, and the moment of escape is gone. His sharp jawline and dark hair make him look like he belongs in a magazine spread, but the shadows under his eyes tell a different story. He's watching me over his coffee cup, reading me like one of his car manuals - methodical, searching for problems to fix.

Theo sits across from him, grinning and waving like he hasn't seen me in days instead of yesterday. His light brown hair is its usual mess, looking more like he just finished a workout than heading to work. I drag my feet across the room, dropping into the seat across from them.

"You're late," Theo says, his broad shoulders shifting as he leans forward. "We almost sent a search party."

"Hey," I mumble, pretending to study the menu I've memorized. Anything to avoid Gray's steady gaze.

"You look tired," Gray says, his tone carefully neutral.

"Thanks for that." The words come out sharp, defensive. He doesn't flinch, just takes another slow sip of coffee.

Theo props his chin on his hand, blue eyes crinkling at the corners. "Ignore him. He's just mad because they ran out of scones."

Gray shoots him a look that would wither anyone else, but Theo just grins wider. "Seriously, though," he says, voice softening. "How are you holding up?"

"I'm fine." The lie rolls off my tongue with practiced ease. I hate how natural it feels.

Before Gray can challenge this obvious untruth, the door chimes and Jace strolls in like he owns the place. His blonde hair is a mess, flour dusting his shirt like he's been in a baking war. The morning light catches his golden skin as he slides into the seat next to me, close enough that I can smell vanilla and coffee on him.

"Morning," he says, flashing that trouble-maker's grin. "You look like you've been avoiding us."

"I have." My deadpan response only makes his grin wider, that damned dimple appearing on his left cheek.

The banter picks up from there, Theo and Jace trading quips while Gray occasionally cuts through with dry commentary. I don't join in, but their familiar rhythm washes over me, almost soothing. Almost.

The air changes when Rhett appears in the doorway, Wes a shadow behind him. Conversations around us dim slightly - Rhett has that effect, commanding attention without trying. His dark auburn hair catches the light as he scans the room, his broad frame filling the doorway. Behind him, Wes moves with that predator's grace of his, all lean muscle and sharp angles in his usual black. Where Rhett draws eyes, Wes seems to slip between them, noticed only when he wants to be.

The easy mood evaporates as Rhett stops at our table, jaw tight. "We need to talk," he says, voice quiet but carrying that fire-captain authority he never quite shakes off.

"Nice to see you too," Theo tries, but Rhett's focus is locked on me.

Wes settles next to Gray without a word, dark eyes taking everything in. There's concern there, hidden beneath his carefully neutral expression. It makes my stomach twist.

"What's going on?" I ask, though part of me already knows.

"Your landlord," Rhett says, and something in his voice makes me go cold. "I saw him outside your building last night."

My stomach drops. The café suddenly feels too warm, too crowded. "It's fine," I say quickly. "He didn't—"

"It's not fine." Rhett's voice is deceptively calm, but I recognize the rage simmering underneath. "That guy's a problem, Bree. He was just standing there, watching your window like he was waiting for something." His hands clench on the table. "Or someone."

The change in the group is instant. Gray sits up straighter, coffee forgotten. Theo's easy smile vanishes, replaced by something harder. Even Jace goes still beside me, his usual restless energy coiling into something dangerous. Wes leans forward, his calculated stillness more threatening than any movement.

"It's handled." I hate how my voice shakes, betraying the lie. "I don't need you guys swooping in every time something happens."

"We're not swooping in." Rhett's eyes lock onto mine, green fire burning there. "We're watching out for you. There's a difference."

The weight of their concern crushes down on me. Five sets of eyes, five different versions of worry and protective anger. It's suffocating. Overwhelming. Too much.

"I don't need this," I mutter, but the words sound weak even to me.

Silence stretches between us, heavy with everything I won't say. Everything they want to say.

Finally, Rhett sighs, but there's no defeat in it. "We're not letting this go, Bree."

"Neither should you." Wes's quiet words cut deepest because he rarely speaks without purpose. His dark eyes hold mine, seeing too much, understanding too well. Like he knows exactly why I'm running, why I keep pushing them away.

And maybe he does. Maybe they all do. That's what scares me most.

Gray's eyes haven't left me since I snapped at him, dissecting every twitch, every breath. The worry in his gaze burns worse than anger would.

"You don't have to keep staring at me," I mutter, focusing on the scratched table surface. Years of stories are carved here—initials, hearts, random words etched by hands that needed somewhere to put their pain. I get that now more than ever.

Gray takes his time responding, each second heavy between us. "I'm trying to figure out what's going on in that head of yours."

"There's nothing to figure out." The lie tastes bitter, worse than the cold coffee.

Theo leans in, his gaze steady, his words measured. "Come on, Bree. We're just worried. You've been... different lately."

"I've been busy." Even I don't believe it anymore.

"With what?" Rhett's voice cuts through the café noise like a blade. "Your landlord?"

The words hit like a physical blow, sending heat rushing to my face. "What the hell is that supposed to mean?"

The table goes silent. Even Jace, who can joke his way through a funeral, freezes. Gray opens his mouth, probably to smooth things over, but Rhett beats him to it.

"That's not—" he starts, his tone carefully neutral, but something in me snaps.

"Do you think I'm sleeping with him?" My voice rises, trembling with rage and something darker. Heads turn at nearby tables, but I'm past caring. My chest feels too tight, like I'm trying to breathe underwater. "Because if that's what you're implying, just fucking say it."

Rhett leans forward, his green eyes dark with something that might be hurt. "I didn't say that."

"You didn't have to." My nails dig into the table edge, anchoring me against the storm building in my chest. The wood grain blurs as tears threaten.

"Bree—" Gray's voice carries that tone, the one that means he's about to be reasonable, about to make sense of things I can't face.

"You think you can just sit there and judge me?" The words taste like acid. "Like you've got it all figured out? I don't need this from you. Not from any of you."

Gray shifts closer, his voice gentle but relentless. "We're not judging you. We just—"

"I know," I cut him off, the words sharp enough to make the couple at the next table flinch. Heat crawls up my neck as I lower my voice. "I know you're trying to help. But I've got it under control."

"Do you?" Wes's quiet question slices through my defenses like they're paper.

I whip around to face him, meeting that steady, unblinking stare. His calm feels like an accusation. "Excuse me?"

He doesn't flinch. "You keep saying you've got it under control, but all I see is you shutting us out."

The truth in his words hits hard leaving me scrambling. "I... I don't need—"

"What?" Rhett's voice is taut, stretched thin over worry and frustration. "You don't need us? You don't need anyone?"

"I don't." The words explode out of me, too loud, too raw. They hang in the air between us, sharp enough to draw blood. The silence that follows presses against my chest until I can't breathe.

I shove back from the table, my chair screeching against the floor. "I've got to get to work."

"Bree—" Theo reaches for me, but I'm already moving.

"Don't." My voice cracks on the single word. My hands shake as I grab my bag, clutching the strap like it's the only thing holding me together. "Just... don't."

The cheerful bell above the door mocks me as I escape into the morning air. Behind me, I can feel their eyes, their concern, their disappointment. It follows me down the street, a weight heavier than my scrubs bag.

# Chapter 4
## BREE

The brick facade of Maple Grove looms ahead like a fortress, a welcome distraction from the weight of their eyes still burning into my back. Here, at least, I know what to do. Here, I can be useful without anyone trying to fix me. The antiseptic smell hits as I push through the doors, mixing with the artificial floral air freshener they use to mask the underlying scents of age and decline.

"Morning, Bree." Sarah's tired smile matches the bags under her eyes as she looks up from the reception desk.

"Morning." I manage to lift the corners of my mouth, though my face feels like it might crack from the effort.

I throw myself into the routine: checking vitals, changing beds, helping with medications. Mrs. Henderson needs help with her knitting. Mr. Jacobs is having one of his bad days, confusion clouding his eyes as I guide him back to his room. I talk him through it, my voice steady even as my own thoughts spiral.

"Bree?" Mrs. Henderson's voice pulls me back to the present. Her hands tremble as she works with her yarn, but her eyes are sharp when they meet mine. There's something knowing in her gaze that makes me want to look away.

"Yes, Mrs. H?"

"You remind me of my daughter." She says it softly, like she's sharing a secret. Like she can see right through me.

The words catch me off guard, lodging somewhere between my ribs. "I do?"

"She was always so strong." Her voice carries a hint of pride tinged with sadness. "Even when things were hard, she kept going. You're like that, you know? Always taking care of everyone else."

I force another smile, but it feels brittle on my face. My chest tightens as I think of the guys, of how I pushed them away this morning. Some kind of caretaker I am. "Thanks, Mrs. H. That means a lot."

But as I step into the hallway, her words follow me like ghosts. Strong. The thought almost makes me laugh. I'm not strong. I'm just really good at running away, at pushing away the people who actually give a damn about me.

By the time my shift ends, the sky has swallowed the sun whole, and the streets are quiet. The air feels heavier than usual as I make my way home, the faint glow of the streetlights casting long shadows that remind me too much of my father's silhouette in a doorway.

The mist starts to stir as I turn the corner to my apartment. It curls around my feet, cool and insistent, like it's been waiting for me. Like it knows what kind of night this is going to be.

"What do you want?" I whisper, my voice barely audible. The words hang in the air between us, heavy with everything I'm trying not to re-member.

The mist drifts at the edges of my vision as I turn the corner to my apartment, hovering like a distant observer. Like always. Sometimes I wonder if

I'm imagining the way it seems to follow me, the way it lingers in doorways and shadows.

I fumble with my keys, the metal cold against my shaking fingers as I unlock the door to my shoebox apartment. The Ridge, as I mockingly call it, greets me with its familiar musty smell and oppressive silence. The air feels stale, trapped, just like me. Home sweet home, right?

Dropping my bag by the door, I kick off my shoes and shuffle to the kitchenette. The linoleum floor creaks beneath my feet, each step a weary sound that matches the hollow ache in my chest. God, I was such an idiot this morning. The guys were just trying to help, and I pushed them away. Again. Like always. Because that's what I do best, isn't it?

I grab a mug from the cupboard, carefully avoiding the chipped one that says *World's Best Daughter*. The irony stings every time. The coffee maker sputters to life, its rhythmic dripping a poor substitute for the warmth of real conversation, for the connection I keep throwing away like it's somehow going to protect them.

As I wait for my liquid lifeline, I lean against the counter and close my eyes. Gray's concerned face flashes in my mind, followed by Wes's furrowed brow and Rhett's sharp words. Theo's quiet understanding, Jace's forced smile—they'd all been there, trying to bridge the gap I keep forcing wider. They'd be better off without me, I tell myself again. I'm just dragging them down, a constant reminder of a past they're trying to escape. A broken thing they can't fix, no matter how hard they try.

The coffee maker beeps, jarring me from my spiral of self-loathing. I pour the steaming liquid into my mug, the bitter aroma filling my nostrils. It's a small comfort, but I'll take what I can get. It's more than I deserve anyway.

Cradling the warm mug in my hands, I shuffle to the couch. My gaze falls on the old, worn journal still on the coffee table. Something tugs at me—maybe it's masochism, or maybe it's just the need to punish myself further for pushing away the only people who still give a damn about me.

With a resigned sigh, I set down my coffee and reach for the journal. The leather is soft under my fingers, worn smooth by years of desperate scribbling. I flip it open to a random page, my heart sinking as I recognize the date at the top.

**July 15th.**

I was twelve.

My hands tremble as I read the first line, written in the shaky handwriting of a child whose world had just been shattered.

*"Daddy came into my room tonight. He said we were going to play a special game, just the two of us."*

The words blur as tears fill my eyes, but I force myself to keep reading. Every detail is seared into my memory, but seeing it on the page makes it real in a way my nightmares never could. The fear, the confusion, the pain—it's all there in black and white.

I read about how I curled up in the corner of my bed afterward, clutching my stuffed bear and praying for my mom to come home. But she never did. She was already gone by then, swallowed up by whatever took her away from us.

My breathing is shallow, my chest tight as I snap the journal shut, the sound echoing in the oppressive silence of the apartment. My stomach churns, and for a moment, I think I might be sick. I press my hands to my face, willing the tears to stop, but they fall anyway, hot and relentless.

The mist hovers near the window, a faint presence at the edge of my awareness. Watching. Always watching. I turn away from it, shoving the journal under the coffee table. Out of sight, out of mind. Or so I tell myself.

But the weight in my chest doesn't lift. It presses harder, heavier, until I can't fight it anymore. My legs give out, and I sink to the floor, my back against the couch. The tears come again, slower this time, as I hug my knees to my chest.

The room feels too quiet, too empty. The ache spreads, clawing its way through every inch of me until I feel hollow, like I'm barely here. The walls press in, the silence growing teeth.

"I can't do this anymore," I whisper into the darkness, my voice cracking. The words fall flat, swallowed by the stillness. Through the window, the mist shifts and swirls, like it's trying to reach me. Its familiar coolness brushes against my skin, but even that comfort feels wrong tonight. Everything feels wrong.

My limbs grow heavy as exhaustion drags me under. The couch digs into my shoulder, the floor hard beneath me, but I don't move. Can't move. The mist thickens around me, its presence both soothing and suffocating. Like it knows something I don't. Like it's trying to tell me something I'm not ready to hear.

I close my eyes, letting the tears dry tacky on my cheeks. The last thing I notice before sleep claims me is how the mist seems to pulse in rhythm with my breathing, wrapping around me like a shroud. Like a promise. Or maybe a warning.

# Chapter 5
## BREE

A week. Seven whole days of silence since I woke up on that floor, muscles stiff and eyes swollen.

No calls. No texts. Not even a passive-aggressive meme from Jace.

It's what I wanted, isn't it?

The thought swirls in my mind, tangling with the ache in my chest. I press my forehead to the window, watching the rain streak down the glass. My feet throb from another double shift at Maple Grove, but the physical pain is almost welcome—something real to focus on besides the hollow feeling inside. The gray sky feels fitting. Appropriate. It's been a week since I stormed out of Mercer's, and while part of me feels lighter, the rest of me feels... empty.

For the first time in years, they've given me space—real space. I told them to leave me alone, and they listened. I should be happy. Relieved. I should be basking in the quiet, in the freedom of not having anyone else to answer to.

Instead, it feels like there's an invisible thread pulling at me, taut and fraying, waiting to snap.

The week has been a blur of restless nights and too-early mornings. Nightmares have clawed their way into my sleep, leaving me shaken and gasping for air. Each one is the same: shadows creeping in, voices echoing from a past I've worked so hard to bury. My mother's voice. My father's anger. And the mist—always the mist, curling and shifting, a silent witness to it all.

I've thrown myself into work, picking up extra shifts at Maple Grove, distracting myself with Mrs. Henderson's stories and Mr. Jacobs' wandering thoughts. But even there, the quiet moments between tasks leave room for memories to creep in.

The rain drums against the window in a steady rhythm, each drop creating tiny rivers that distort the world outside. It reminds me of tears—the ones I won't let fall anymore.

Even with the silence, they're still here

Gray's sharp eyes, always calculating, always seeing too much. Theo's warmth, his easy grin that could thaw an iceberg. Jace's carefree laugh, hiding a depth he doesn't let many see. Rhett's steady presence, a wall I could lean on if I let myself. And Wes... Wes, with his quiet strength and the way his words always cut right to the heart of things.

I shake my head, tearing my gaze from the rain. No. This is for the best. I told them to stay away because I knew I couldn't keep dragging them into my mess. They don't need my baggage. They deserve better than that—better than me.

But the truth is, I miss them.

Life feels colder without Jace's ridiculous jokes. The quiet is suffocating without Theo's laughter filling the gaps. I even miss Rhett's constant pushback, the way he challenges me in ways no one else dares to.

I cross the room, grabbing the journal from the coffee table. I flip it open, not bothering to find a specific page. The words blur together, fragments of thoughts and memories that feel both familiar and foreign.

**March 3rd, Junior Year.**

*I think if I just disappeared, no one would notice. Would they even care? I tried calling Rhett today. He was with Cindy Matthews—I could hear her laughing in the background when he finally picked up. He said he'd call me back, but he never did. Probably for the best. He doesn't need to deal with my mess anyway. Not when he has someone normal, someone whole.*

I flip the page, my throat tight.

**April 15th.**

*Jace made everyone laugh at lunch today. Even me. For a second, I almost forgot about everything—about Dad, about Mom, about the bruises I had to cover up this morning. He caught me smiling and did this ridiculous victory dance. Sometimes I wonder if he knows how much those moments mean. How sometimes his stupid jokes are the only thing that gets me through the day.*

I snap the journal shut, the sound sharp in the stillness.

Enough.

I toss the journal onto the couch and grab my hoodie from the hook by the door.

I need air.

Space.

Something to shake off the weight pressing on my chest.

The streets are quiet, the city muted under the gray sky. My feet carry me without thought, the familiar route winding toward the park at the edge of the neighborhood. It's a small slice of green in a sea of concrete, and on a day like this, it's empty except for the ghosts of a thousand memories.

*This is fine. I'm fine.*

But even as I tell myself that, the mist stirs at the edges of my vision, curling around the base of the bench like smoke from a forgotten cigarette.

It's funny how this place always feels like a bubble, separate from everything else. I used to come here when I was a teenager, back when home felt like a cage and school wasn't much better. Back when I still believed running away could fix anything. The guys would find me here sometimes—Jace with his pockets full of stolen candy bars, Gray with his silent understanding, Rhett pretending he'd "just happened" to be passing by.

A shiver runs through me as another memory surfaces, unbidden but vivid.

I was sixteen, sitting right here on this very bench. The late afternoon sun was warm on my skin, the air heavy with the smell of freshly cut grass. A boy—Daniel—sat beside me, too close. His knee bumped against mine, and I shifted away, but he only leaned closer.

"You're so pretty, Bree," he murmured, his hand brushing my arm. I froze, my stomach twisting. "I bet you've never even been kissed, huh? You're not gonna say no to me, are you?"

I did. Of course I did. But he didn't care. His hand moved to my thigh, and panic exploded in my chest. I shoved him, harder than I thought I could, and scrambled to my feet.

"Don't touch me!" My voice cracked, loud and shrill, drawing a few curious glances from passersby.

Daniel stood too, his face a mix of anger and embarrassment. "What the fuck, Bree. Don't be such a tease. What's your problem?"

He grabbed my wrist, yanking me toward him. The sharp sting of his slap came before I even realized what was happening. My cheek burned, hot tears stinging my eyes, but I refused to let them fall. Refused to give him the satisfaction.

"Hey!" The voice was sharp, cutting through the fog of shock and fear.

I turned, and there he was. Theo. His broad frame filled my vision, his usually light expression hard and unyielding. I'd never seen him look like that before, and I haven't since.

Theo didn't ask what happened. He didn't need to. He just stepped between us, his body a wall of protection. "You need to leave," he told Daniel, his voice low but dangerous.

Daniel tried to bluster, muttering something about it being a misunderstanding, but Theo didn't budge. He just stood there, his blue eyes blazing, until Daniel finally backed down and slunk away.

"You okay?" Theo asked, turning to me. His voice softened, the tension in his shoulders easing.

I nodded, even though I wasn't. "Yeah. Thanks."

He didn't push. He just sat with me on the bench until the sun dipped below the horizon, neither of us saying much. It was the kind of quiet I needed—the kind that didn't demand anything from me.

Back in the present, I blink, my hand tightening around the strap of my bag. The memory fades, but the ache in my chest lingers. I haven't thought about that day in years, but sitting here, it feels as raw as it did then. That's the thing about the guys—they've always been there, stepping in when I needed them most, even when I couldn't admit I needed anyone.

Theo didn't know what I'd been through. Not really. None of them did. But they'd seen enough to know I needed someone, even if I couldn't ask for it. And now... now I've pushed them so far away, I'm not sure they'll ever come back.

The sound of children's laughter pulls me back to the present. I glance around, taking in a family that brought two little ones to play in the rain. It's peaceful here, but it doesn't feel like it used to. Nothing does.

With a sigh, I stand and head home, my feet dragging against the path. The weight of the past clings to me like a shadow, one I can't seem to outrun.

When I reach my apartment, the sight of the daisy stops me cold. It's lying on the doormat, simple and unassuming, yet so out of place against the peeling paint of the door and the stained concrete hallway. Perfect white petals, like the ones that used to appear on my windowsill when I was fifteen, when everything felt darkest.

For a moment, I just stare at it, my mind spinning. It doesn't make sense. Who would leave this here? There's no note, no explanation, just a flower.

My chest tightens as I crouch to pick it up, the delicate petals trembling slightly in my fingers. A memory flashes before I can stop it - me at sixteen, curled on my bed after Dad kicked me down the stairs. The pain in my ribs made it hard to breathe, but worse was the hopelessness, the certainty that this was all my life would ever be.

Then I saw it on my windowsill. A single daisy, laid there as carefully as this one. Perfect white petals catching the morning light. I never figured out who left it, but for a moment, the weight in my chest had lifted. Someone had seen me. Someone had cared enough to leave this small piece of beauty.

Other daisies appeared after that, always when things felt darkest. Always when I needed them most. But I never caught who left them. Never let myself hope too hard about what they meant.

A memory flashes: Gray, walking past my window every morning on his way to school, never saying a word. Rhett, always watching, always noticing when I wore long sleeves in summer. Theo, with his careful questions that never pushed too far.

Could this be them? Did one of them leave it? Or is this just some weird coincidence, another piece of the universe's cruel sense of humor?

I shake my head, pressing the flower to my chest as I unlock the door. Inside, the apartment feels even smaller than usual, the familiar mustiness pressing down on me. The mist stirs faintly at the edges of the room, curling toward me like it knows I need the company. I sink onto the couch, the daisy still in my hand, and stare at it.

It's probably nothing. Just a random flower, dropped by someone passing through. That's the logical explanation, isn't it?

But what if it's not?

The thought lodges in my mind, stubborn and impossible to ignore. My fingers trace the soft petals as I turn the daisy over, again and again. It doesn't make sense. None of it does. But for the first time in a week, I feel something other than the crushing weight of my own thoughts.

It's just a flower. Small. Insignificant. But it feels like a question. A whisper that maybe, just maybe, I haven't burned every bridge.

I place the daisy on my coffee table, impossibly white against the dark wood. In the fading light, it almost seems to glow, like the hope I'm trying so hard not to feel. The mist lingers at the edges of my vision, quiet and watchful, as constant as the guys have always been—even when I wish they weren't. Even when I tell myself I don't deserve them.

I don't tell it to go away. Instead, I let it be, just like I let myself remember, just for tonight, what it feels like to be seen.

# Chapter 6
## BREE

My shift is quieter than usual tonight, a welcome relief after a week of restless nights and lingering exhaustion. The dining room is almost empty as I clear the last plates, the familiar routine almost peaceful until I notice Mrs. Henderson's missing from her usual spot by the window. She never misses dinner.

I'm stacking the dishes when a scream shatters the silence.

"Help! Someone, help!"

The plate slips from my hands, ceramic hitting linoleum with a crash that echoes the way my heart slams against my ribs. I run toward the sound, my feet carrying me before my mind can catch up. Rounding the corner, I skid to a halt, my breath catching in my throat.

Mrs. Henderson lies crumpled on the floor, her wispy white hair spread across the linoleum like it's reaching for something unseen. Her skin is too pale, her hand outstretched toward something I can't see. Just like Mom that last morning, reaching for something in the dark before she vanished—

No. Focus.

For a moment, the world seems to stop. My legs lock, my chest tightening with a familiar, suffocating weight.

"I called 911!" a voice shouts, jolting me back into motion.

I drop to my knees beside her, ignoring the sharp pain as they hit the floor. My hands tremble as I reach for hers, clutching them tightly, willing warmth back into her cold fingers. "Mrs. Henderson," I say, my voice steady despite the panic clawing at me. "It's Bree. I'm here. Just hold on."

Her pulse flutters beneath my fingertips, weak but present. Like a bird trying to break free.

The sound of running footsteps pulls me back. Everything blurs into motion after that - the paramedics arriving, their movements swift and precise as they work. Someone asks about family contacts. The question hits like a physical blow: she has no one.

"I'll go with her," I hear myself say, my voice thin but determined. "She shouldn't be alone."

The hospital smells like antiseptic and rain-soaked pavement. I sit slumped in a plastic chair, my hands gripping each other tightly in my lap. The hours blur together as I wait, the buzz of fluorescent lights making my head throb. I don't know how long I've been here, but when the nurse approaches, I already know what she's going to say.

"She's gone," the nurse tells me gently. "She passed peacefully."

They're words meant to comfort, but they don't. I stayed with her, held her hand as her breaths grew shallow, and told her it was okay to let go. But as I sit there now, the hollowness feels unbearable.

"You didn't have to stay," the nurse adds kindly, her hand on my shoulder. "Most people don't."

I shrug, my voice barely a whisper. "Someone should have."

The words feel small, like they don't hold enough weight for the moment. But it's all I can offer.

The rain greets me as I step outside, cold and relentless. My hoodie does little to shield me from the downpour, but I don't care. The mist begins to curl faintly at my feet, its presence familiar yet unsettling. It's like an unspoken reminder of how broken I really am.

Mrs. Henderson's last moments replay in my head as I walk. The softness of her grip, the shallow rise and fall of her chest. I told her she wasn't alone. I hope she believed me.

My building looms in the distance, dark and foreboding. As I draw closer, something feels off. My steps falter when I spot the figure leaning against the wall near the entrance, too still to be casual.

Phil.

My stomach twists. His silhouette is unmistakable even in the dim light, and his posture—loose and swaying—screams trouble. I consider turning around, taking the long way, but I know it won't matter. He'll wait.

"Bree," he calls out, his voice slurred and thick. He pushes off the wall, swaying slightly as he moves toward me. "Been waiting for you."

I clench my fists, forcing my voice to stay steady. "It's late, Phil. Go home."

He ignores me, stepping closer. "Can't leave you out here all alone," he says, his grin predatory. "Not safe for a pretty thing like you."

The mist lingers at the edges of my vision, faint and unmoving. My chest tightens, my pulse pounding in my ears. "I'm home," I say flatly. "You should leave."

Phil's grin fades, replaced by something colder. "You don't talk to me like that," he snaps, his voice low and sharp. "You think you're better than me? Huh?"

Before I can react, his hand shoots out, gripping my arm hard enough to bruise. Panic explodes in my chest. I twist, trying to pull free, but he's too strong. "Let go!" I yell, my voice breaking.

The mist shifts faintly, a cold presence that wraps around my ankles. The air around us seems to thicken, and Phil's grip slackens just enough for me to wrench free. His eyes dart around wildly, his breathing ragged.

"What the fuck is that?" he mutters, his gaze unfocused. He stumbles back, his face pale and drawn, like he's seeing something I can't.

I don't wait. I run.

The rain obscures the streetlights as I put distance between us, my breath coming in ragged gasps. My soaked hoodie clings to me, the cold biting through to my skin. I'm too exhausted to think, too shaken to stop.

I can't stop the tears that blur my vision and mix with the rain on my face. My lungs burn, but I push on, driven by a primal fear that overrides everything else. The mist swirls around my feet, matching my frantic pace, a silent companion in my flight.

Phil touched me. He put his hands on me. The thought loops in my mind, each repetition sending fresh waves of panic through my body. I can still feel the ghost of his grip on my arm, the alcohol on his breath, the predatory gleam in his eyes. It's too much like before, too close to memories I've tried so hard to bury.

I don't know where I'm going, just that I need to get away. The streets blend together, unfamiliar in the darkness and the rain. My clothes are soaked through, and I'm shivering, but I can't tell if it's from the cold or the fear that's taken root in my chest.

Headlights sweep across me from behind, and my heart stutters. A truck slows beside me, the engine's rumble too close, too loud. No no no. My legs shake as I try to run faster, but my feet slip on the wet pavement. The driver's door opens, and I stumble backward, ready to bolt down the nearest alley.

"Bree."

The voice cuts through the rain, through the panic. I know that voice. But I can't—I can't trust it. Can't trust anything right now. I back away, shaking my head, my vision swimming.

"Bree, stop." Closer now. Steady. Like an anchor I don't deserve.

I finally look up, really look, and there's Rhett, moving toward me with careful steps. Those green eyes I know so well take in every detail—my trembling hands, my soaked clothes, the way I can barely stand. His gaze catches on my torn sleeve, the exposed skin underneath already darkening where Phil's fingers dug in. His jaw tightens, something dangerous flashing across his face.

"What happened?" he asks, his voice softer now, but his fists are clenched at his sides.

"I'm fine," I whisper, the words automatic and hollow. But they crumble as tears spill over, hot and relentless against the cold rain.

Rhett's hands hover, unsure but wanting to reach for me. "Bree," he says, his voice firm yet kind, "you're not fine. Let me take you somewhere safe."

I shake my head, the thought of my apartment making me sick. "I don't want to go back there."

His jaw tightens. "Okay," he says, his tone steadying. "You don't have to. Just get in the truck."

I hesitate, Mrs. Henderson's death and Phil's attack crashing over me in waves until I can barely stand. But Rhett's presence anchors me, just like it always has. When I finally climb into the passenger seat, he closes the door with careful gentleness, the same way he used to speak when my father was on a rampage, soft and steady like he could somehow shield me even through those thin apartment walls.

The warmth of the truck seeps into my bones as Rhett slides behind the wheel. The mist swirls briefly at my feet before fading away. He doesn't ask questions - he never does. Just drives, one hand steady on the wheel, the other resting on the console between us. An offer, not a demand.

For the first time all night, the weight in my chest eases just enough to breathe.

# Chapter 7
## UNKNOWN

The rain falls softer now, but she's finally safe. My magic trembles, drained and unsteady after what I had to do. I wasn't even certain I could affect her realm so directly—the distance between us makes every intervention dangerous, unpredictable. But when that man touched her, when I felt her fear spike through the mist like lightning...I had to try.

The effort leaves me weak, vulnerable. Even now, I can barely stand, my connection to the mist flickering like a candle in wind. But watching her climb into the mortal's truck—Rhett, she calls him—makes the sacrifice worth it.

She's so much stronger than she knows. So much more than these shadows she hides in. The mist recognized her power long before I did, drawn to her light like a moth to flame. Even now it curls around her, protective, possessive.

Soon. Soon she'll understand what she is. What we could be. The mist chose us—marked us for each other long before I knew her name.

But for now, I let my consciousness fade from her realm, my grip on the mist loosening. The last thing I see is her hand, trembling but steady, reaching for the comfort he offers. It sends an ache through my chest—familiar, expectant. These mortals care for her, protect her in their limited way. For that, I'm grateful.

*Rest, little flame. Your guardians will watch over you until we can be together again.*

# Chapter 8
## BREE

The silence wraps around us like a blanket as Rhett drives, broken only by the rhythmic swish of windshield wipers and the soft patter of rain. I stare out the window, but I'm not really seeing anything. My mind keeps circling back to Phil's grip on my arm, to Mrs. Henderson's last breath, to the way the mist seemed to respond when...

I squeeze my eyes shut. I can't think about that right now.

"Almost there," Rhett says quietly, and my stomach clenches as I realize where we're heading. The truck turns onto Oak Street, lined with old Victorian homes split into apartments. I've gone past their place a hundred times but never went inside. Another wall I built. Another boundary I enforced.

Rhett pulls into a narrow driveway beside a huge blue Victorian, complete with a wraparound porch and way too many windows. Light spills from several of them, warm and inviting in a way that makes my chest ache. A shadow moves past one of the first-floor windows—probably Theo, he's always up late reading.

He hesitates, his hands tightening on the wheel before he finally speaks. "You don't have to come in. I can call you a cab, or take you anywhere else you want to go."

My throat tightens, the weight of the offer pressing down on me. I should say yes. I should ask for a cab, go somewhere—anywhere that won't make this night more complicated than it already is. But I'm so tired. Tired of running, tired of being afraid, tired of being alone.

I take a shaky breath. "Okay."

Rhett's head turns, his eyes flicking to mine as if he's checking to see if I really mean it. When I don't say anything else, he nods and pushes the door open. He's around to my side of the truck in an instant, but he doesn't touch me. He just holds the door and waits as I slowly uncurl myself from the seat.

My legs shake as I follow him up the porch steps. The old wood creaks beneath our feet, and I catch the scent of rain-soaked cedar. Rhett unlocks the door, and warmth spills out—along with the smell of coffee and something else, something that smells like cinnamon and safety.

"Just for tonight," I say, my voice rough. "Just until..."

Until what? Until I'm less broken? Less afraid? Less me?

Rhett's eyes soften, but he just nods. "Just for tonight."

Rhett nudges the door shut behind us, locking it with a quiet click. The warmth of the house hits me immediately, and with it, the overwhelming realization of how cold I am. My damp clothes cling to me, my fingers frozen stiff.

"Let me grab you a towel or some clothes," Rhett says, his voice low, steady. He glances at me like he's afraid I'll bolt the moment he moves.

I nod faintly, crossing my arms tighter around myself. But before Rhett can step away, the sound of footsteps on the stairs makes us both freeze.

Theo rounds the corner, a book in hand, his head down as he reads. He stops mid-step, his foot hovering over the last stair when he looks up and sees me. His face shifts instantly—surprise, worry, and something else I can't quite name flashing through his blue eyes.

"Bree?" His voice is soft, careful, like he's afraid I'll shatter if he speaks too loud. "What... are you okay?"

I open my mouth, but no words come out. My throat feels too tight. Theo sets the book down on the banister and takes a cautious step forward, his brows knitting together as he studies me.

I know what he sees. The damp hoodie clinging to my frame, the dark circles under my eyes, the way my arms are wrapped so tightly around myself it's like I'm trying to hold myself together.

And suddenly, I can't stand it. The worry in his eyes, the quiet way he looks at me like I'm some fragile thing he needs to fix. My chest tightens with the familiar sting of shame.

"I'm fine," I mumble, though the words sound hollow even to me. "Sorry... I didn't mean to—"

"Don't," Theo interrupts gently. "Don't apologize."

I swallow hard, dropping my gaze to the floor. My mind starts spiraling, berating myself for letting things get to this point. For making them worry. Again.

"I'll be right back" Rhett murmurs as he leaves the room. Theo steps closer, his movements slow and deliberate, like he's trying not to spook me. "Come on," he says softly, tilting his head toward the hallway. "Let's get you warmed up."

I nod again, my legs moving on autopilot as he guides me down the hall. The warmth of the house presses against my damp clothes, a reminder of how cold I still feel. The soft sound of voices drifts through the air, and I stiffen when I hear someone call out.

"Theo, is that you? There's snacks!" Jace's voice is light and teasing, but the knot in my chest tightens. Snacks. The idea of food should be comforting, but all I feel is the gnawing ache of shame.

I glance at Theo, ready to make an excuse to leave, but before I can speak, my stomach growls loudly, betraying me. My cheeks burn as I wrap my arms tighter around myself, hoping the sound wasn't as loud as it felt.

Theo raises an eyebrow, his lips twitching like he's trying not to smile. "Guess we're heading to the kitchen," he says gently, not giving me a chance to argue.

The kitchen is warm and bright, its mismatched cabinets and cluttered counters making it feel inviting in a way that catches me off guard. Jace is leaning against the counter, a half-empty bag of chips in one hand, while Gray stands near the sink, his arms crossed.

Both of them turn as we enter, their expressions shifting the moment they see me. Jace's easy grin falters, replaced by something softer, and Gray's sharp eyes narrow as they sweep over me, cataloging every detail. I feel their scrutiny like a weight, heavy and suffocating.

"Bree," Gray says, his voice calm but tight, like he's holding back a tidal wave of questions. His sharp eyes scan me like he's reading every shadow under my eyes, every tremor in my hands. I hate it.

Jace tries to lighten the mood, as always. "Hey, didn't expect to see you tonight." He holds up the bag of chips, his grin wobbly. "Want some? They're stale, but, you know, free food."

I manage a weak smile, but my throat is too tight to answer. Before I can find my voice, Theo nudges me toward a chair at the table and drapes a blanket over my shoulders. The soft fabric is warm, but it feels like too much, like a weight pressing down on me.

Gray's voice cuts through the quiet. "What happened?"

My chest tightens, my fingers gripping the edges of the blanket as if it might anchor me. "It's nothing," I mumble, my voice barely audible. "I'm fine."

"Bullshit." The word is quiet but firm, and Gray steps closer, his green eyes locking on mine. "You're not fine."

"Gray," Theo warns, his voice low, but Gray doesn't back down.

"You show up here in the middle of the night, soaked to the bone, and you're saying it's nothing?" His tone isn't angry—it's sharp with concern, cutting through the fragile wall I've built around myself. "Talk to us, Bree. Let us help."

I freeze, my mind scrambling for a way out. The air feels too thick, the room too warm, their concern too much.

"You're right," I say, my voice tight as I push back from the table. "I should go."

Jace's eyes widen, and Theo moves to stop me, but I'm already standing. The blanket slips from my shoulders and pools on the floor as I turn toward the hallway. My heart pounds, the overwhelming urge to escape drowning out the voices in the room.

I take a shaky breath.

*I need to go. I can't stay here. Not like this.*

I make it two steps before Rhett appears, holding a towel and a neatly folded t-shirt and boxers. He stops mid-step, his brows drawing together as he takes in the scene. His eyes flick from the dropped blanket to my trembling hands.

"Where are you going?" he asks, his voice calm but firm enough to make me pause.

"I shouldn't be here," I say, the words tumbling out in a rush. "This was a mistake. I'm fine. I can—"

"Bree." Rhett steps closer, setting the towel and clothes on the back of a chair. His voice is steady, unwavering. "Stop."

The single word cuts through the noise in my head, and I freeze, my fingers curling into fists at my sides. I glance at the door, then at the floor, the weight of his gaze holding me in place.

"You don't have to do this," Rhett says, softer this time. "You don't have to run."

The fight drains out of me all at once, leaving me sagging under the weight of my own exhaustion. My throat tightens, and I blink hard, willing the tears to stay where they are.

"You're not a burden," Rhett continues. His tone is low, deliberate. "And you don't have to go through this alone."

Something in me cracks, just a little.

# Chapter 9
## RHETT

The house feels wrong tonight. Not the usual kind of quiet that settles in after a long day, when we're all winding down in our own ways. This is heavier—sharp with unspoken words and the kind of tension that makes my shoulders ache. My damp shirt still clings to my skin from the rain, but I can't bring myself to leave the kitchen long enough to change.

Jace leans against the counter, a glass of water clutched in his hand like he's forgotten it's there. His eyes haven't left Bree since she sat down, and I get it. She looks small, huddled at our kitchen table with Theo's blanket wrapped around her shoulders. The way she's holding herself—tight, closed off—it's like she's trying to disappear into herself. I've seen that look before, back when we were kids. It never meant anything good.

I catch Theo's eye and he nods, understanding without words. He's always been good at that.

"Come on, Bree," he says, keeping his voice soft like he's talking to a spooked animal. "Let's get you cleaned up. You can take the guest room tonight."

She hesitates, fingers tightening around the blanket's edge. For a second, I think she's going to bolt—that instinct to run written all over her face. But then she nods, movements stiff like she's forcing herself to stay put.

Theo guides her toward the stairs, careful not to touch her, and something in my chest aches at how natural that caution has become.

The moment they disappear down the hall, I let out a breath I didn't realize I was holding. The weight of responsibility settles deeper on my shoulders, familiar but heavy.

"Well," Jace mutters, breaking the silence, "this has been a shit night."

Gray finally moves from his spot by the sink, his crossed arms and sharp eyes reminding me of how he looks when he's diagnosing a particularly stubborn engine problem. "She needed to hear it."

"Did she?" Jace's voice is sharper than usual, the usual warmth stripped away. He sets the glass on the counter and crosses his arms, the movement jerky. "Because from where I'm standing, it looks like you practically shoved her out the door."

Gray stiffens, his jaw tightening. "She's not going to let us help if she keeps pretending everything's fine. Someone had to push."

"Push?" Jace scoffs, that restless energy of his turning sharp. "You think cornering her into a breakdown is helping? Come on, Gray."

"Enough." I don't raise my voice—don't need to. They both turn to me, that simmering frustration hanging between them like smoke. "We're all on edge, but fighting isn't going to fix this."

Jace mutters something under his breath but doesn't argue further. Gray's gaze flicks toward the staircase, and I can see the doubt creeping into his expression. He's replaying what happened, just like the rest of us are.

The sound of the front door opening and closing breaks the quiet. Wes walks in, his dark curls damp from the rain, his expression neutral but sharp. He stops in the doorway, his dark eyes sweeping over the room before landing on the glass of water sitting untouched on the table.

"What the hell is going on?" he asks, his voice low.

I rub the back of my neck, feeling every hour of this endless night. "Bree's here," I say simply. "She's upstairs with Theo."

Wes's brow furrows. "Why?"

"She had a rough night," Jace says, deflating a bit. "Rhett brought her back."

Before Wes can ask anything else, Theo reappears, his steps slow as he comes back down the stairs. He looks at me first, then at the others, his expression a mix of exhaustion and something softer. "She's out," he says, leaning against the banister. "Passed out as soon as her head hit the pillow."

"Good," Jace mutters, shaking his head. "She needs it."

Theo doesn't move to sit. Instead, he turns to Gray, his blue eyes steady but hard. "What the hell was that back there?"

Gray stiffens. "I was trying to help."

"Help Bree? Or your own curiosity?" Theo's voice is quiet but pointed, each word sharp enough to cut. "She's already hanging by a thread, and you thought pushing her was the right call?"

"She wasn't going to talk otherwise," Gray snaps back, his tone defensive. "She keeps shutting us out—"

"And maybe there's a reason for that," Jace cuts in, but his voice lacks its usual heat. He runs his hands through his hair, frustrated. "Look, I saw the bruise when she came in, the torn sleeve. Something happened—something bad—and Gray's not wrong. She's not going to tell us shit unless we push." He laughs, but there's no humor in it. "But she's not like you, man. She doesn't process things by turning them into puzzles to solve."

Theo leans against the banister, his gaze steady but tired. "She barely said anything upstairs," he murmurs. "When I asked if she was okay, she just... brushed it off. Like even admitting something's wrong is too much for her right now." He exhales slowly, his hands gripping the banister as if grounding himself. "She's not just shutting us out because she's stubborn. She's shutting us out because she doesn't think she can let us in."

Gray shifts, his jaw tightening as he stares down at the floor. His foot scuffs lightly against the tile, the sound small but loud in the silence. "I get it, okay? I shouldn't have pushed. But I can't just stand here and watch her fall apart."

"We're all watching her fall apart," I say, stepping in before the argument spirals further. "But if we're going to help her, we can't keep pulling in different directions."

The room falls into a tense silence, each of us lost in our own thoughts.

"She doesn't trust us anymore," Theo says finally, his voice quieter. "I don't know what we did, but she feels like she's alone. We have to be patient."

"That's not going to be easy," Jace mutters, shaking his head. His fingers tap a restless rhythm on his bicep as he shifts again, glancing toward the stairs like he's hoping she'll magically reappear and prove them all wrong.

"Nothing worth doing ever is," Wes says simply, his voice calm but firm. He leans against the doorway, his dark eyes flicking toward the stairs like he's already thinking three steps ahead.

I glance toward the stairs, the weight in my chest settling deeper. "She's here now," I say quietly. "That's a start."

# Chapter 10
## BREE

*Darkness presses in on all sides, suffocating and endless. The only sound is my heartbeat, loud and frantic, echoing in my ears like a drum. Then, faintly, a voice cuts through the silence.*

*"Bree."*

*I freeze, every muscle locking up as the voice grows louder, closer.*

*"You're such a lucky girl, Bree. Daddy needs you."*

*No.*

*"Show daddy what you can do, Princess."*

*I want to scream, to fight, to run. But my body betrays me, frozen in terror as his weight settles onto the mattress. His hands are rough, calloused, uncaring as they paw at me. There's no tenderness, no attempt to make it anything but an act of selfish taking.*

*The pain is sharp, invasive. I bite my lip until I taste blood, desperate to stay silent. To make a sound is to make it real, to acknowledge that this is happening again.*

*He grunts, his breath hot and sour against my neck. I retreat deep inside myself, imagining I'm anywhere but here. When it's over, he leaves without a word, as if I'm nothing more than a convenient object to be used and discarded.*

I curl into myself, shame and revulsion coursing through me. *This is what love looks like,* I think bitterly. *This is all I'm good for.*

The memory fades, but the visceral feeling of violation lingers. I jolt awake, my chest heaving and my body trembling. The room around me is quiet, the soft gray light of dawn filtering through the curtains. For a moment, I forget where I am.

Then it all comes rushing back. The hospital. The rain. Phil. Rhett.

I sit up slowly, my heart still hammering against my ribs. Sweat makes my borrowed clothes cling to my skin as I try to orient myself. The room swims into focus—cozy, lived-in, with mismatched furniture and a faint smell of pine and old books. Theo's blanket is draped over the foot of the bed, and there's a pile of neatly folded clothes on the chair near the door—probably Rhett's, judging by the size.

My stomach twists. I shouldn't be here.

The ghost of the nightmare still clings to me, its shadow stretching into the corners of my mind. Phil's leering face from last night superimposes itself over my father's, a grotesque overlap of different men and the same entitled cruelty.

My skin crawls, and I have the overwhelming urge to scrub myself raw. But no amount of soap can wash away the stain of these memories, the way they've twisted my perception of intimacy and trust.

I slide out of bed, wincing as my bare feet touch the cool floor. The soreness in my arm from Phil's grip pulls me back into the present. I glance at the neatly folded clothes again, the quiet thought that Rhett's trying to make me feel at home flickering and fading as quickly as it came.

I shouldn't stay.

They don't need me. They don't need this.

I don't belong here.

The thought settles like a weight in my chest as I grab the clothes and change quickly, pulling the soft t-shirt over my head. It smells like cedar and something clean, and for a second, it feels like a hug I don't deserve. I push the thought away.

The house is quiet as I creep down the stairs, each creak of the wood making me wince. My breath catches as I reach the living room. The front door looms ahead of me, like a lifeline.

Almost there.

I reach for the doorknob, but a voice cuts through the stillness, low and steady. "You weren't planning on saying goodbye, were you?"

I freeze, my hand hovering over the doorknob. Slowly, I turn, my heart sinking when I see Wes sitting in the armchair near the window. His dark eyes are sharp but calm, his posture relaxed like he's been waiting for this.

"Wes," I murmur, my voice barely audible.

He leans forward slightly, resting his elbows on his knees. "It's early," he says simply. "Where are you going?"

"I..." My throat feels tight. "I need to go. I shouldn't have stayed."

His gaze doesn't waver, and the silence stretches, heavy and expectant. "Why not?"

"Because..." The words stick, and I swallow hard. "Because I don't belong here. You guys don't need this—don't need me."

Wes stands slowly, his movements unhurried but deliberate, and steps closer. "Is that what you think? That you're a burden?"

I look away, my fingers tightening around the strap of my bag. "It's not what I think. It's what I know."

His sigh is quiet, almost imperceptible, but the weight of it presses against me. "Bree, we've been friends our whole lives. You know us. Do you really think we'd let you go through this alone?"

I shake my head, biting the inside of my cheek to keep the tears at bay. "I don't want to drag you into my mess."

"You're not dragging us into anything," he says firmly. "We're already here. Whether you want us to be or not."

"He's right."

The voice cuts through the stillness, making me jump. I spin around to see Gray standing in the hallway, his green eyes sharp and unreadable. He leans casually against the doorframe, but there's nothing casual about the way he's looking at me.

"You're not dragging us into anything," Gray continues, stepping closer. "And you're not doing anyone any favors by pretending we don't care."

I take a step back, the strap of my bag slipping slightly from my shoulder. "I'm not pretending—"

"Yes, you are," he interrupts, his tone unwavering. "You've been doing it for years. And you're damn good at it. But you don't get to shut us out anymore, Bree. Not after last night."

The words hit harder than I expect, knocking the air out of my lungs. "You don't understand," I whisper. "You don't know what it's like—"

"Then tell us." Gray's voice softens, but the intensity in his gaze doesn't waver. "Help us understand. Let us in."

"Gray," Wes says, his tone a quiet warning.

But Gray doesn't back down. "She needs to hear this."

I stare at him, my chest tightening. "I can't."

"Yes, you can," Gray says, taking another step forward. "We're not going anywhere, Bree. No matter how hard you try to push us away, we're still here."

The weight of his words press down on me, the truth of them both comforting and terrifying. I feel the tears welling up, but I blink them back, refusing to let them fall.

"I should go," I murmur, but even I can hear how hollow the words sound.

"No," Wes says gently but firmly, stepping beside Gray. "You should stay."

The two of them stand there, a united front against my instinct to run. My legs feel heavy, weighted by something that feels like exhaustion but might be surrender.

# Chapter 11
## BREE

Steam clouds the small bathroom, curling around the mirror and softening the harsh light overhead. I let the hot water cascade over me, my muscles aching with relief as I lean against the cool tile wall. The heat seeps into my skin, washing away the rain, the cold, and the lingering feeling of Phil's grip on my arm.

I stayed.

The thought circles in my mind, startling every time it surfaces. I stayed. I didn't bolt.

*What the hell is wrong with me?*

I squeeze my eyes shut, trying to focus on the steady rhythm of the water hitting the tub. It's safer to think about that than the fact that I'm standing here in their house, using their bathroom, doing exactly what I promised myself I wouldn't do.

A lump forms in my throat, and I bite it back. It's not like they're mad I stayed. If anything, they wanted me to. Wes and Gray practically said as much.

Wes's calm assurance echoes in my mind. "We're already here, whether you want us to be or not."

My chest tightens, the weight of his words pressing against my ribs. They're here. Always have been. And I've been pushing them away for years, convinced it was better for everyone.

I run my hands over my arms, scrubbing harder than necessary, as if I can scrub away the thoughts with the grime. Just like my scars.

The mirror is completely fogged over when I step out, and for a moment, I stare at my hazy reflection. The girl in the mirror looks softer, less jagged around the edges. Maybe it's just the steam, but she doesn't look like she's been running for as long as I feel like I have.

I pull the towel tighter around me and turn away before I can think too much about it.

Stepping out of the bathroom, dressed again in Rhett's borrowed clothes, I hesitate in the hallway. The sound of voices drifts up from downstairs—lighthearted, full of life. My stomach does a slow flip, equal parts longing and dread. Pots clink, and the faint smell of coffee and something sweet wafts through the air.

For a second, I consider retreating back to the room. Curling up under the blanket Theo left me and pretending none of this ever happened. But the warmth of their voices draws me forward, tugging at something fragile inside me.

I pad down the stairs, one hand trailing along the wooden railing. The closer I get to the kitchen, the more distinct the voices become.

"Why the hell are you using every pan we own?" Gray's tone is sharp, but there's no real heat behind it.

"Because I'm making a masterpiece," Jace says, the grin evident in his voice. "Something the lady of the hour deserves."

"It's pancakes, Jace," Rhett deadpans. "Not an art exhibit."

"Pancakes," Theo corrects. "Waffles. Bacon. Eggs. Fruit. You're basically making a buffet."

Jace snorts. "I aim to impress."

"Where did all this come from anyway? I don't think I've ever seen so much food in this house at once." Gray says, his curiosity getting the best of him.

"I went shopping." Jace responds like it's obvious.

I stop just outside the kitchen, wrapping my arms around me, listening to their banter. It's easy, natural, like they've been doing this forever. And they probably have.

Then Jace's voice cuts through the noise. "I swear I heard her upstairs. Think she'll join us, or do I need to deliver the pancakes directly to her room?"

"Leave her alone," Rhett says, though his tone is softer than usual. "She'll come down when she's ready."

I square my shoulders, but I can't help thinking about the loose sleeves of Rhett's shirt falling just above my elbows. They're going to see so much of my skin they haven't seen since we were kids, so much of my past. I try hard to shake away the thought, but the weight of it lingers, pressing down on me as I step closer to the kitchen.

My heart pounds with every step, my bare feet almost silent against the floor. I stop just short of the doorway, clutching my arms to my chest. Their voices fill the space, warm and easy, and I let myself hover in the shadow of the hall, listening.

"Almost done," Jace says, his voice rising cheerfully above the clatter of pans. "Prepare to be amazed, gentlemen."

Gray snorts. "That's a big promise for pancakes."

"They're not just pancakes," Jace says, feigning offense. "These are works of art. Made with love. And maybe some stress."

Theo chuckles softly. "More like showing off."

"Call it what you want," Jace fires back. "But no one's going hungry today, thanks to me."

Rhett's voice cuts in, calmer but teasing. "We'll see if the pancakes make it to the table before you burn them."

For a moment, I just stand there, soaking it in. It feels wrong to step into it, like I'll disturb the balance of something perfect.

Then Jace speaks again, his voice exaggeratedly loud. "Seriously, though. She's gotta be starving after last night. Should I take her some bacon or—"

"Jace," Rhett says, sharper this time. "I'm sure she'll be down."

I take a deep breath and step into the doorway before they can notice me lingering. The room falls quiet for a fraction of a second as their eyes shift to me, and I feel the weight of their attention like a physical thing. I resist the urge to cross my arms over my chest, to hide the parts of me I've never wanted them to see.

"There she is," Jace says, breaking the moment with a wide grin. He's standing at the stove, a spatula in one hand and a pan in the other, his easy confidence barely hiding the flicker of relief in his eyes.

Theo leans against the counter, holding his coffee mug with both hands the way he always does when he's worried, his usual calm smile softening as his gaze meets mine. Gray, perched against the far wall, straightens slightly, his sharp eyes flicking over me while his shoulders stay tense despite his casual stance. Rhett, still sitting at the table, glances up, his expression steady but softening just enough to be noticeable.

"You made it just in time," Jace says, flipping the pancake in the pan with a flourish. "Feast of champions, right here."

I pull the shirt's hem lower, suddenly too aware of my bare legs and the scars they can probably see now. My throat tightens, but I force myself to speak. "You didn't have to do all this."

"Didn't have to," Jace says, grinning. "But I wanted to. That's what friends do, Bree."

The words hit me like a physical blow, gentle but undeniable. Because that's what they've always done, isn't it? Been there, steady and unwavering, while I've spent years convincing myself I didn't deserve it.

# Chapter 12
## BREE

I hesitate at the edge of the room, my bare feet sticking to the cool tiles, but Rhett's steady gaze grounds me. He's the only one at the table, slicing strawberries into neat piles with an ease that makes me ache with something I don't have words for.

"Sit," he says, his tone calm but firm. "I'll grab you some coffee."

Before I can protest, he's already standing, heading for the counter where the pot sits steaming. My legs feel shaky as I move toward the chair nearest to him, pulling Rhett's shirt lower over my legs and crossing my arms against the sudden urge to retreat.

Jace glances over his shoulder from the stove, still brandishing the spatula like a conductor leading an orchestra. "You're gonna love this, Bree. Best pancakes of your life. Guaranteed."

The sound of footsteps draws my attention to the hallway, where Wes appears, moving with that quiet grace of his. His dark eyes meet mine for a moment, and something in his expression tells me he's been waiting, watching to make sure I didn't try to slip away again.

"Morning," he says simply, leaning against the doorframe.

"Morning," I manage, my voice quieter than I mean for it to be.

"Did you save me some of the masterpiece, or are you hoarding it all?" Gray's voice carries from near the coffee pot, his sharp green eyes sweeping the room before landing on me. He doesn't say anything, but the tension in his shoulders eases as he moves to lean against the wall.

"Masterpiece?" Wes asks from his spot by the counter, arching a brow.

"Perfection," Jace corrects, pointing the spatula at him. "And yes, I saved you some. But Bree gets the first plate."

"Lucky me," I murmur, staring at the empty plate in front of me like it might fill itself if I wish hard enough.

The guys settle in one by one, the table filling with movement. Plates clatter, coffee mugs are filled, and Jace's voice carries over everything, filling the space with easy chatter.

Rhett sets a mug of coffee in front of me, the steam curling upward in soft spirals. "Here," he says simply.

"Thanks," I whisper, curling my hands around the warmth.

Jace finally sets a plate in front of me, piled high with pancakes, eggs, and bacon. "Et voilà," he says, grinning.

"It's a lot," I say, my stomach twisting at the sight of so much food.

"You deserve it," Jace replies, sitting down across from me. "We all do."

The table hums with life as the guys start eating, their banter light but steady. For the first time in what feels like forever, I let myself listen—really listen. The sound of their voices, the clink of forks on plates, the soft scrape of chairs against the floor.

It feels normal. Too normal.

I stare at my plate, pushing a piece of pancake around with my fork. The food smells amazing, but my stomach churns every time I try to take a bite. They're all being so careful—too careful. Like I'm made of glass. Like last night never happened.

But it did happen. I'm sitting here in Rhett's borrowed clothes while Phil is probably passed out in his apartment, planning God knows what. While Mrs. Henderson is—

The fork slips from my fingers, clattering against the plate. The sound cuts through the conversation, and suddenly five pairs of eyes are on me. I can feel the weight of their concern pressing in from all sides.

"Bree?" Rhett's voice is quiet, but it carries a current of something stronger.

"I'm fine," I say automatically, but the words feel hollow. Empty. Like everything else I've been telling them.

"You haven't touched your food," Jace says, trying to keep his tone light even though I can hear the worry underneath. "Not up to your standards?"

I shake my head, gripping the edge of the table. "No, it's not—I just—" My throat closes up around the words. How do I explain that I don't deserve this? Their kindness, their concern, their endless patience with my broken pieces?

"You don't have to talk about it," Wes says from his across the table, his voice steady. "But you do need to eat."

Something in me snaps. "Why are you all acting like this is normal?" The words burst out before I can stop them. "Like I didn't show up in the middle of the night, like I'm not wearing your clothes, like—" My voice cracks. "Like everything's fine when it's not. It's not fine. None of this is fine."

The silence that follows feels sharp enough to cut. I stare down at my hands, watching them tremble against the dark wood of the table. My heart pounds so hard I wonder if they can hear it.

"No," Gray says finally, his voice quiet but firm. "It's not fine."

I look up, startled by the edge in his tone. He's watching me with those sharp eyes of his, all pretense of casualness gone.

"None of this is fine," he continues. "You showing up scared in the middle of the night? Not fine. You being afraid to come to us? Not fine." His jaw tightens. "You thinking you have to handle everything alone? Definitely not fine."

"Gray," Rhett warns, but Gray shakes his head.

"No, she needs to hear this." He leans forward, his gaze holding mine. "We're not acting like everything's normal, Bree. We're trying to give you space to feel safe. But don't think for a second that we're okay with any of this."

My throat burns. "I didn't—I wasn't trying to—"

"We know," Theo cuts in gently. "But Gray's right. You don't have to pretend with us."

"And you don't have to run," Wes adds quietly from his seat. "Not anymore."

Jace sets his fork down, all his usual playfulness gone. "What happened last night, Bree?"

The question hangs in the air between us. I wrap my arms around myself, trying to hold in the tremors that threaten to shake me apart. "I can't—" My voice breaks. "Mrs. Henderson died."

The words fall like stones into still water. Ripples of shock cross their faces.

"And then Phil..." I swallow hard, the memory of his grip making my skin crawl. "He was waiting when I got home. He grabbed me, and I couldn't—" My voice cracks again. "I couldn't get away at first."

The mist coils around my feet, cold and agitated, as the room temperature seems to drop. The shift is instant - Jace's fork freezes halfway to his mouth, his knuckles white. Gray goes preternaturally still, like a predator catching a scent. Theo sets his mug down with calculated precision, while Rhett's breath catches in a way that sounds like pain. Even Wes, usually so controlled, straightens with a fluid motion that reminds me of a blade being drawn.

I can't look at any of them, but I feel the change in the air—like a match about to strike.

"He what?" Gray's voice is low, dangerous in a way I've never heard before.

Rhett's chair scrapes against the floor as he stands, but Wes's quiet voice cuts through the tension. "Let her finish."

I squeeze my eyes shut, trying to steady my breathing. "I got away. The mist—" I stop, catching myself. They don't need to know about that part. About how strange it was, how Phil stumbled back like he was seeing something that wasn't there. "I just ran. And Rhett found me."

"I'll kill him." Jace's words are soft, matter-of-fact, like he's commenting on the weather. The fork in his hand trembles slightly, betraying the rage beneath his calm.

"Get in line," Gray mutters, his fingers white-knuckled around his coffee mug.

"Guys," Theo warns, but there's an edge to his voice too. He sets his mug down carefully, too carefully, like he's afraid of what his hands might do if he doesn't control every movement.

"You're not going back there." Rhett's tone leaves no room for argument. When I look up, his eyes are fierce, protective in a way that makes my chest ache. "We'll get your things today."

"I can't just—" The words stick in my throat as reality crashes back in. "My lease. The rent. I can't afford—"

"Stay here," Wes says simply.

My head snaps to him. "What?"

"Stay here," he repeats, leaning forward. "We have the room. You know we do."

"I—" The offer hits me like a physical blow. "I can't."

"Why not?" Theo asks softly.

Because I don't deserve it. Because I'll ruin everything. Because—

"Because I'm scared," I whisper, the truth slipping out before I can stop it.

The word hangs in the air between us—scared. Such a small word for something that feels like it's crushing my chest. I stare down at my untouched plate, waiting for them to laugh, to brush it off, to tell me I'm being ridiculous.

But they don't.

"Of what?" Theo asks gently, his voice soft enough that I have to look up. His blue eyes are steady, patient in a way that makes my throat tight.

"Everything," I whisper, the truth spilling out before I can stop it. "Of letting you down. Of being too much. Of—" I swallow hard, wrapping my arms tighter around myself. "Of ruining everything."

"Bree." Gray's voice is rougher than usual. When I glance at him, his jaw is tight, like he's fighting back words. "You couldn't ruin anything if you tried."

A bitter laugh escapes me. "You don't know that."

"Actually, we do." Jace sets his fork down, all his usual playfulness gone. "We've known you our whole lives, remember? Through everything. And you've never ruined a single thing."

"That's different," I say, my voice cracking. "This is—living here would be different."

"Why?" Wes asks simply, his dark eyes intent. "Because you couldn't hide from us anymore?"

The question hits like a physical blow. I flinch, but he doesn't back down.

"That's it, isn't it?" he continues, his voice gentle but unwavering. "You're scared because we'd see everything. All the parts you try so hard to keep hidden."

Tears burn behind my eyes. "You don't want that," I whisper. "Trust me."

"Don't tell us what we want." Rhett's voice is quiet but firm. He leans forward, his green eyes burning with an intensity that makes my breath catch. "We want you safe. We want you here, where we can protect you."

"I don't need protecting," I say automatically, but the words sound hollow even to me.

"Bullshit." Gray's response is sharp enough to make me jump. "Phil got close enough to grab you. To hurt you." His hand shoots out toward the bruise peeking out of the shirt sleeve. "That's not happening again."

"And what about next time?" The words tumble out, bitter and afraid. "What happens when something else goes wrong? When I wake up screaming from nightmares? When I can't—" My voice breaks. "When

I can't handle being touched, or when I just need to be alone? When everything becomes too much?"

"Then we'll be there," Rhett says quietly. "However you need us to be."

I shake my head, pressing my palms flat against the table to stop them from shaking. "You don't understand. I don't know how to do this."

"Do what?" Jace asks.

"Let people in. Let you help. I've spent so long trying to keep everything locked away, trying not to be a burden—"

"Stop." Rhett's voice cuts through my spiral. "You're not a burden. You've never been a burden."

"But—"

"No." He reaches across the table, his hand stopping just short of mine. An offer, not a demand. "You're family, Bree. You always have been. Let us be there for you, the way you've always been there for us."

The tears I've been fighting finally spill over. "I don't know how," I whisper again, but this time it's not a refusal. It's a plea.

"Then we'll figure it out together," Theo says softly. "One day at a time."

# Chapter 13
## JACE

"So, where's the moving truck?" I ask, leaning against Rhett's pickup. The morning sun beats down on the cracked parking lot of Bree's apartment complex, making the air shimmer like a mirage. It's the kind of heat that usually has me cracking jokes about melting, but today feels different. Heavier.

Bree shifts uncomfortably beside Gray, her keys clutched tight in her hand. She's drowning in one of Rhett's old hoodies, and something about that makes my chest ache. "We don't need one," she says quietly.

"Come on," I grin, trying to keep things light. "Everyone needs a moving truck. How else are we gonna haul your furniture? Your books? Your—"

"Jace." Theo's voice carries a warning, but I'm already trailing off as I catch the look on Bree's face.

She won't meet any of our eyes as she moves toward the building's entrance. "It won't take long," she mumbles. "I don't have much."

The stairwell smells like stale cigarettes and regret. Each step creaks under our feet, the sound echoing off grimy walls. I try to think of something funny to say—it's what I do, right? Keep things light, keep everyone smiling. But the words stick in my throat as I watch Bree climb ahead of us, her shoulders hunched like she's trying to make herself smaller.

Third floor. No elevator. Because of course there isn't.

Bree stops at her door, and I notice how her hand shakes as she fits the key into the lock. The handle sticks, and she has to jiggle it just right—the kind of thing you learn from doing it a thousand times. Behind me, I hear Gray's sharp intake of breath. *Yeah, buddy. I feel that too.*

The door swings open with a groan that makes my teeth ache. Bree steps inside first, and we follow like a funeral procession. The thought makes me want to laugh, but the sound dies in my chest as I take in her apartment.

It's... empty. Not the kind of empty that comes from packing things up. Just empty. Like she never really moved in at all.

The lumpy couch sags against one wall, its fabric worn thin in spots. A coffee table that's seen better decades sits in front of it, covered in water rings and what looks like old burn marks. There's no TV, no pictures on the walls, nothing that makes a place feel like home.

"Bree," Theo breathes, and there's so much in that one word it makes my chest hurt.

She wraps her arms around herself, still not looking at any of us. "I told you it wouldn't take long."

I scan the room again, trying to find something—anything—that says this is where our Bree has been living. But there's just... nothing. A few boxes stacked neatly in the corner. Some books. A journal on the coffee table.

"Where's your—" I start, then stop, not even sure how to finish that sentence. Your life? Your things? The proof that you existed here?

"This is it," she says quietly, and fuck if that doesn't hit me like a punch to the gut.

Rhett moves first, crossing to the boxes with that quiet intensity of his. His jaw is set in a way that means he's grinding his teeth—a habit he picked up in firefighter training. He needs to do something, to fix this, but there's nothing to fix. Just empty space and too many questions.

Gray hasn't moved from the doorway. His eyes are sharp, cataloging everything—or rather, the lack of everything. I know that look. He's putting pieces together, and I can tell by the tension in his shoulders that he doesn't like the picture they're making.

"The kitchen—" Wes starts, taking a step toward it, but Bree cuts him off.

"Don't." Her voice cracks. "Please."

But he's already looking, we all are, and Jesus Christ. One plate. One mug. A handful of utensils. The kind of setup you'd have in a motel room, not a home.

"How long?" Gray's voice is too quiet, too controlled. "How long have you been living like this?"

Bree shrugs, the movement small and defeated. "Does it matter?"

"Yes." The word comes out sharper than I mean it to. "Yes, it fucking matters."

She flinches, and I immediately hate myself for it. But I can't help it. This is Bree. Our Bree. The girl who used to help me with my homework even when she was dead tired from her own. The one who always made sure we ate during finals week. Who took care of everyone but herself.

And we let this happen.

"Okay," Theo says, and thank God for him because someone needs to be practical right now. "Let's start with the boxes."

He moves toward them, and I follow because it's something to do with my hands that isn't punching walls. As I lift the first box—light, too light—I catch movement by the window. For a second, I think I see something shimmer in the air, like heat waves rising from asphalt. But when I blink, it's gone.

Probably just the sun playing tricks. Has to be. Because the alternative—that I just saw the same mist that's been following Bree since we were kids—that's not something I'm ready to think about.

Not yet.

Lifting the boxes is almost worse than seeing them. Each one feels like a confession—how little she has, how much she's been hiding. I can hear the others moving around the studio behind me, their silence heavy with things none of us know how to say.

"You've got books," I try, aiming for light as I peer into one of the boxes. "That's good. Theo was worried we wouldn't have enough nerdy stuff in the house."

The joke falls flat, especially when I see what else is in the box. A worn teddy bear, its fur matted and one ear torn. I recognize it immediately—she's had it since we were kids. Since before her mom left. My throat gets tight as I realize this box probably holds everything she couldn't stand to lose.

Everything that survived her father.

"Where do you sleep?" Gray asks suddenly, his voice tight as he takes in the empty space. There's no bed, not even a mattress. Just that lumpy couch that looks about as comfortable as concrete.

Bree wraps her arms around herself. "The couch folds out," she mumbles, but we all hear what she's not saying. That ancient thing probably hasn't folded out properly in years.

I move to the closet—the only other storage space in the tiny studio—and my heart sinks further. A few sets of scrubs hung neatly on wire hangers. Two regular outfits that I recognize because she's worn them so many times. A pair of pajamas folded on the shelf above. That's it. That's her whole wardrobe.

"The lease," Gray says, turning to Bree. His voice is carefully controlled, but I can see how white his knuckles are where he's gripping the closet door. "How much do you owe?"

She shakes her head. "I can handle it."

"Bree." His voice carries that edge we all know too well. "How much?"

"Two months," she whispers, staring at the floor. "But I'll figure it out. I always do."

Always do. The words hit me like a freight train. How many times has she been in this situation? How many times has she had to "figure it out" while we were all busy with our lives, thinking she was fine just because she said she was?

"I've got it," I say, the words coming out before I can think about them. When she starts to protest, I hold up a hand. "Nope. Not negotiable. Consider it back rent for all the times you helped me pass calculus."

"Jace—"

"He's right," Theo cuts in smoothly. "Though I think chemistry was more my territory."

"You all helped," she says, her voice small. "You don't owe me anything."

"That's not how family works," Rhett says quietly, and something in his tone makes her finally look up.

I watch the tears well in her eyes before she blinks them back. She's trying so hard to hold it together, to keep those walls up, but they're crumbling. We can all see it.

"Hey," I say, crossing to her. I stop just short of touching her, remembering how she flinches sometimes. "Remember when we were kids, and you used to smuggle extra cookies to Gray because his dad never bought any?"

A ghost of a smile touches her lips. "You knew about that?"

"'Course we did. You weren't exactly subtle, short stack." The old nickname slips out naturally, and for a second, she looks so much like that little girl—the one who took care of all of us even when she had nothing—that my chest aches. "Let us return the favor. Please."

The mist—or whatever it is—moves again by the window, catching my eye. This time I'm sure I'm not imagining it. It curls around Bree's feet like a cat seeking attention, and I swear the air gets heavier, charged with... something.

But now isn't the time to bring that up. We've got other ghosts to deal with first.

# Chapter 14
## BREE

The last box sits on the floor near the door, smaller than the others but heavier with meaning. My journal, photos, ticket stubs from concerts we went to together, silly notes passed in class, pressed daisies - every reminder of the family I've been pushing away. My hands tremble as I pick it up.

"I'll take this one," I say quickly, cutting through the quiet hum of the room. Rhett glances at me, brow furrowed. "It's small. I've got it."

He hesitates but doesn't argue. I slip out before anyone can question it, clutching the box like a shield as I hurry down the stairs. The stairwell's sour smell hardly registers - I just need to get this to the truck before they can ask what's in it.

I push through the door into the bright morning sun, blinking as my eyes adjust. Relief floods through me at the sight of Rhett's truck waiting in the lot.

"Well, well." The voice stops me cold. "Moving out so soon?"

Phil emerges from the shadow of the building, cigarette dangling from his fingers. The mist coils around my ankles, sharp and cold like a warning. His eyes rake over me in that way that makes my skin crawl, that makes me feel small and dirty and trapped.

"Don't," I warn, but my voice shakes.

He grins, flicking ash onto the pavement. The ember glows too bright in the morning sun. "What's wrong, sweetheart? Daddy issues making you run again?"

The words hit hard, making me flinch. I try to step around him, but he moves faster than he should for someone who reeks of alcohol at ten in the morning. His arm shoots out, catching me around the waist and spinning me until my back hits the rough brick wall. The box tumbles from my hands, contents spilling across the concrete.

"Get off me." I push against his chest, but he just presses closer.

"Your daddy said you'd play hard to get." Phil's breath is hot against my face, making my stomach roll. "But he promised me you'd come around. Said it runs in the family - how you pretend you don't want it." His fingers dig into my hip as he leans closer. "That's why I gave you such a good deal on rent. Your old man assured me you'd be a sure thing, just like you were for him."

His words hit me like a punch to the gut. As Phil grinds against me, I feel the sickening evidence of his arousal pressing into my hip. My skin crawls, revulsion coursing through every cell of my body. I want to scrub myself raw, to burn away the memory of his touch.

"Let her go." Rhett's voice cuts through the air like a thunderclap.

Phil's head snaps up, but he doesn't release me. If anything, his grip tightens. "Well, if it isn't the cavalry." His lips curl into an ugly smile. "We're just having a friendly chat about family matters. Right, Bree?"

The way he says 'family' makes acid burn in my chest. Through the haze of panic, I see them - the guys at the base of the stairs, but something's different. Wrong. The easy way they usually carry themselves is gone, replaced by something darker.

Gray's stillness is absolute, the kind that comes before an explosion. Jace's ever-present smile has vanished, leaving something sharp and dangerous in its wake. Theo's usual calm calculation has hardened into cold fury. And Rhett... Rhett looks ready to tear Phil apart with his bare hands.

But it's Wes who moves first.

One moment he's standing with the others, and the next he has Phil by the throat, ripping him away from me with a force I didn't know he possessed. The mist surges with him, cold and sharp like winter's bite. Phil stumbles, gasping, as Wes shoves him against the opposite wall. Even the air feels different - charged with the kind of quiet violence that Wes usually keeps buried deep.

"You think we don't know who you are?" Wes's voice is barely recognizable, stripped of its usual quiet control. Each word drips with carefully contained rage. "What you are?"

"Get your hands off me," Phil snarls, trying to push back, but Wes doesn't budge.

"You touch her again," Wes says, his voice dropping to something that makes even me shiver, "and they won't find enough of you to identify."

"Wes." Theo's voice carries a warning, but his eyes are cold as he moves to gather my scattered belongings.

Phil laughs, but it's shaky. "What are you gonna do? Beat me up? That's assault, buddy."

"No." Gray steps forward, his movement deliberate as a hunter stalking prey. "Assault is what you just did to her. What you tried to do the other night. The police might be interested in hearing about that. Or maybe the housing authority should know about your habit of attacking tenants?"

Phil's face drains of color. "You can't prove anything."

"Wanna bet?" Jace's voice is stripped of its usual warmth. He holds up his phone, screen glowing. "Security camera right there, asshole. Got a nice clear shot of everything."

Wes's grip tightens, and for a second, I think he might actually do it - might actually hurt Phil. The air feels heavy, charged with violence barely contained.

"Wes." My voice comes out smaller than I mean it to. "Don't. Please."

Something in my tone reaches him. He releases Phil with a shove that sends him stumbling. "Get out of here," Wes growls. "If I ever see you near her again..."

He doesn't finish the threat. He doesn't need to.

Phil scrambles away, his bravado crumbling as he nearly trips over himself to get to his car. The screech of tires on pavement echoes through the lot as he peels out.

The silence that follows feels like glass about to shatter, broken only by my shallow breathing. My legs feel strange, disconnected, like they might give out. The brick wall scrapes against my back as I slide down it, barely registering the pain.

*They heard. They know.*

The thought circles in my head, over and over, as black spots dance at the edges of my vision. Years of careful walls, of keeping that part of my life locked away where it couldn't touch them, crumbling because of Phil's drunken taunts.

Someone moves toward me—Theo, I think, but everything's blurry. The world tilts sideways, sounds growing distant like I'm underwater. I'm vaguely aware of voices, of hands hovering near but not touching.

"Bree." Rhett's voice seems to come from far away. "Breathe, sweetheart. Just breathe."

I try, but my chest is too tight. The morning sun feels too bright, too harsh. My skin crawls where Phil touched me, phantom sensations that make my stomach heave.

"—going into shock," I hear Theo say, his voice clipped with barely contained rage. "We need to—"

"Don't touch her," Gray cuts in sharply. "Not yet."

He's right. The thought of hands on me, even theirs, makes panic claw up my throat. I press my palms flat against the rough concrete, trying to ground myself in the sensation.

The mist swirls at my feet, agitated and heavy. Through the fog in my mind, I notice Jace watching it, his face hard with understanding. They can see it too. One more secret exposed.

"Home," Wes says quietly, but his voice still carries that dangerous edge. "We need to get her home."

Home. The word echoes strangely in my head. I want to laugh, or maybe scream. Instead, I just sit there, staring at the scattered contents of my box—my secrets spread out on the pavement like broken glass.

*They know. They know. They know.*

The thought circles like a vulture as black spots dance at the edges of my vision. Years of careful walls crumbling because of Phil's drunken taunts. The mist thickens around me, trying to hold me up as my legs give out, but it's too late. Everything feels distant, underwater, wrong.

The morning sun fractures into pieces, too bright, too harsh. The concrete scrapes my palms as I try to ground myself, but even that feels far away.

The last thing I see is the mist, curling protectively around my scattered secrets on the pavement, before darkness claims me completely.

# Chapter 15
## RHETT

The drive home is too quiet. Behind me, Theo cradles Bree's head in his lap, his fingers hovering near but never touching her hair - always careful, always holding back. Gray sits rigid in the passenger seat, his jaw working silently, teeth grinding loud enough I can hear it over the engine. The rest follow in Wes's car, steady in my rearview mirror, staying close like they're afraid we'll all disappear if they let us out of their sight.

My hands clench around the steering wheel until my knuckles go white, focusing on the smooth leather under my palms instead of the rage burning through my chest. The image of Phil's hands on her keeps flashing through my mind, mixing with his words about her father until I taste copper from biting my cheek too hard. A dull throb starts behind my eyes - the kind of headache that comes from holding yourself together when everything in you wants to break something. Someone.

But I can't lose it. Not now. Not when she needs us steady. Not when she's finally letting us help, even if it took her collapsing for it to happen.

"She's still out," Theo murmurs from the back seat, his voice tight with the kind of control that comes from years of practice. "But her breathing's even."

Gray doesn't turn around, but his shoulders tense at Theo's words. "The mist," he says, voice low and careful. "You all saw it?"

Nobody answers. We don't need to. We'd all watched it swirl around her feet, agitated and heavy, like it was responding to her distress. Just like we used to see when we were kids, though we never talked about it then either.

The house looms ahead, dark windows reflecting the mid-morning sun. I pull into the driveway, and Wes parks behind us, blocking us in. It's what we do now—layers of protection, keeping her surrounded.

"I've got her," I say as I kill the engine, but Theo's already shaking his head.

"Your hands are shaking," he says quietly. "Let me."

He's right. I hadn't even noticed, but my fingers tremble as I release the steering wheel. Jace appears at Theo's door, opening it with uncharacteristic silence. The mist follows as Theo lifts Bree, careful and slow, like she might shatter if he moves too fast.

She looks small in his arms, drowning in my borrowed hoodie, her face pale against the dark fabric. Something in my chest twists at the sight. How many times had she been hurt while we weren't looking? How many secrets has she been carrying alone?

"Inside," Wes says from behind us, his voice carrying that dangerous edge it gets when he's holding himself together by a thread. "Before the neighbors start asking questions."

We move as a unit, falling into an unconscious formation we've perfected over years. Theo carries her, his training evident in every careful step. Wes and Gray flank him like shadows, their movements synchronized without a word passing between them. Jace takes point, already pulling out his keys, while I bring up the rear, watching everything, everyone. We don't need to discuss it - each of us knowing our role, our place in this protective circle we've built around her.

The morning sun streams through the windows as we file inside, catching dust motes in its beam, making everything feel too bright, too normal for what just happened. My throat tightens at how small she looks in Theo's arms, drowning in my borrowed hoodie, her face too pale against the dark fabric.

"Should we take her to…" Jace starts, but Theo cuts him off with a quiet "Guest room." Gray's already heading up the stairs, moving ahead to clear the path, to check every corner like he's done since we were kids and he first heard the sounds through their shared wall. Like he can protect her from everything if he just moves fast enough, plans well enough.

I catch Jace's wrist as he moves to follow. "The box," I murmur. "Her things—"

"On it." He's gone before I can finish, slipping back outside to gather what Phil scattered. What she tried so hard to keep private.

The silence feels heavy as we climb the stairs, broken only by the soft thud of careful footsteps. The mist follows, curling around our ankles, drifting up the bannister like water flowing uphill. None of us mention it. Not yet.

Theo lays her on the bed with a gentleness that makes my chest ache. She looks younger like this, vulnerable in a way she never lets us see when she's awake. Her dark hair spills across the pillow, and I notice the faint tremor in Theo's hands as he steps back.

"She's freezing," he says, voice rough.

Wes moves to the closet, pulling out extra blankets—the ones we bought because Bree's always cold, even if she never admitted it and had never been here to use them. Gray takes them wordlessly, draping them over her with precise movements, tucking the edges like he's building a fortress around her.

"Someone should stay," Wes says, though we all know none of us are leaving. "In case she—"

"Wakes up scared," Gray finishes. "Disoriented."

"Or tries to run," Theo adds quietly.

The truth of it sits heavy between us. Because that's what Bree does—she runs. Has been running for years, we just didn't know from what. Until now.

Jace appears in the doorway, the battered box cradled in his arms like something precious. His face is harder than I've ever seen it, all his usual humor stripped away. "Photos were scattered," he says, voice tight. "And her journal—"

"Don't," I cut him off. The idea of reading her private thoughts, even accidentally, feels like another violation. "Just... put it somewhere safe."

He nods, setting the box carefully on the dresser. We all pretend not to notice how his hands shake, how he has to grip the edge of the dresser for a moment to steady himself.

"Her father," Gray says suddenly, the words sharp enough to make us all flinch. "All this time. Her father—"

"Not now," Theo interrupts, but his voice lacks its usual calm. "We can't... not here. Not with her..."

He doesn't finish, but he doesn't need to. We can all see the mist thickening around Bree, responding to something even in her unconscious state.

"Theo's right," Wes says, his quiet voice carrying an edge of steel. "We deal with that later. Right now—"

"We protect her," I finish. It's what we've always done, even if we failed more times than I can count.

The silence stretches, broken only by Bree's soft breathing. I sink into the armchair by the window, unable to tear my eyes away from her face. She looks peaceful now, but I can still see the moment she collapsed, the way her legs gave out as the truth of Phil's words hit her.

"We should have known." Gray's voice is barely audible, but it carries enough self-loathing to fill the room. He stands by the dresser, fingers tracing the edge of her journal box without touching it. "All those years, living right next door. I heard—" His voice catches. "I heard things. Through the wall. But I never..."

"We all missed it," Theo says, but the words sound hollow. He sits on the floor, back against the wall, looking more undone than I've ever seen him. "Or maybe we didn't want to see it. Because seeing it meant—"

"Admitting we couldn't stop it," Wes finishes. He hasn't moved from his spot near the door, like he's standing guard. The mist swirls around his feet, and for a moment, I swear it takes the shape of something protective, something fierce.

Jace paces near the foot of the bed, that restless energy of his turned sharp and dangerous. "Phil said her father promised him—" He cuts himself off, hands clenching into fists. "They were talking. Recently. About her."

The implications hit like a physical blow. Her father isn't just some ghost from her past. He's still out there, still trying to control her, still—

"We find him." Gray's voice has gone cold, calculated. "We find both of them."

"And do what?" Theo asks, though there's something in his tone that suggests he already has ideas. Dark ones.

"Whatever we have to," Wes says simply.

I watch the mist curl higher around the bed, like it's responding to our anger, our need to protect her. "First," I say, forcing my voice steady, "we make sure she's safe. Really safe." I look at each of them in turn. "No more letting her push us away. No more respecting boundaries that are killing her."

"She'll fight it," Jace says, finally stopping his pacing. "You know she will."

"Let her," Gray says, and there's something fierce in his voice. "She can hate us for keeping her safe. That's better than—" He swallows hard. "Better than the alternative."

Movement on the bed makes us all freeze. Bree shifts slightly, a small sound escaping her that might be pain or fear. The mist thickens instantly, and I notice how we all lean forward, instinctively ready to move.

But she settles again, fingers clutching the blanket Gray tucked around her. Even unconscious, she's trying to hold herself together.

"We need a plan," Theo says quietly, his analytical mind already working. "For when she wakes up. For after."

"She stays here," I say firmly. "Non-negotiable."

"Agreed," Wes nods. "But that's just the start."

"Her apartment," Gray adds. "We need to clear it out. Today. Make sure Phil can't—" His jaw clenches. "Can't use anything against her."

"I'll handle the lease, like I said." Jace offers. "And maybe have a word with the housing authority about our friend Phil." His smile is sharp enough to cut. "I'm sure they'd be interested in his business practices."

"Carefully," Theo warns. "We can't risk him running to her father if we spook him too badly."

The thought sends a chill down my spine. Her father. The monster who lived next door to us for years. Who hurt her while we played video games and complained about homework. Who's still hurting her, even now.

"One thing at a time," I say, even though every cell in my body screams for immediate action. For violence. "Right now, we focus on her. On making sure she knows..."

"That she's not alone," Wes finishes. "Not anymore."

The mist shifts again, almost like it's agreeing. Like it's been waiting for us to finally understand, to finally see what's been right in front of us all along.

"We should talk about that too," Theo says carefully, his eyes tracking the mist's movement. "About what we saw. What we've always seen but never discussed."

The mist coils thicker around Bree's unconscious form, almost like it's listening. Like it knows we're finally acknowledging what we've spent years pretending not to notice. A sound escapes her - small, wounded - and the temperature in the room seems to drop as the mist responds instantly, wrapping around her like a shield.

The protective surge isn't just from the mist. I catch Gray's hand twitching toward her, see Wes shift his weight like he's ready to move, notice how Jace's restless energy stills completely. We're all connected to her by threads we can't explain, drawn to protect her in ways that go deeper than friendship or even love.

"Later," I say, watching how the mist moves, how it mirrors our need to keep her safe even now. "Everything else can wait. Right now, we just..." The words catch in my throat, thick with everything I can't express.

"We stay," Gray finishes simply, his voice carrying the weight of a vow.

So we do. Because it's all we can do. All we've ever done, even when we didn't understand why she pulled at us like gravity. Even when we failed her.

Not again. Never again.

# Chapter 16
## BREE

Awareness comes in fragments. The softness beneath me isn't my lumpy couch. The blankets are too heavy, too warm. Even through closed eyelids, the light feels wrong—softer somehow, filtered through curtains I don't own.

Then memory crashes back. Phil. The box. His words about my father. *They know.*

My chest constricts as panic claws up my throat. They know everything. Every secret I've kept locked away, every wall I've built—gone. Shattered like the careful lies I've been telling for years.

I force my eyes open, then immediately wish I hadn't. The room spins slightly, but I recognize it—the guest room at their house. The one I slept in last night, with its soft gray walls. The one that was supposed to be mine, but I push that thought away.

The mist hovers at the edges of my vision, thicker than usual. Almost... protective? I blink hard, trying to clear it away before anyone notices.

A soft exhale draws my attention to the armchair by the window. Rhett sits there, his head tipped back, eyes closed. But even in sleep, his jaw is clenched tight. One hand rests on the chair arm, fingers curled like he's ready to move at any moment.

Gray leans against the wall near the dresser, arms crossed, watching me with those sharp eyes that see too much. My battered box sits on the dresser behind him—the one that held every memory I tried to keep safe. The one Phil scattered across the concrete like worthless trash.

My journal. *Oh god, my journal.*

"We didn't read it," Gray says quietly, as if reading my thoughts. "We just... gathered everything up. Put it somewhere safe."

I try to sit up, but my arms shake too much to support my weight. Before I can try again, Theo appears at my side, his movements careful and measured.

"Easy," he murmurs. "You've been out for a while."

The door opens, and Wes slips in like a shadow, followed by Jace. They move with an unfamiliar tension, all of Jace's usual lightness gone, Wes's quiet energy turned sharp.

Five pairs of eyes watch me, heavy with things I'm not ready to face. With knowledge I never wanted them to have.

"How much..." My voice cracks. I swallow hard and try again. "How much did you hear?"

"Enough." Rhett's voice is carefully controlled, but I can hear the rage simmering beneath it. He sits forward, elbows on his knees, and the morning light catches the shadows under his eyes. "Why didn't you tell us?"

The question hits like a physical blow. I curl my fingers into the blankets, anchoring myself against the tide of shame threatening to pull me under.

"I couldn't." The words come out small, broken. "I didn't want you to know. To see..."

"To see what?" Theo asks gently. "That you were hurting? That you needed help?"

A bitter laugh escapes me. "To see how weak I am. How broken. How much I deserved it."

"Stop." Gray's voice cuts through the air like a blade. "You're not weak. You're not broken. You're—" He breaks off, his hands clenching at his sides. "You survived. You protected everyone but yourself. That's not weakness, Bree. That's strength."

The tears spill over, hot and relentless. "You don't understand. He's still... he can still..."

"He can't touch you." Wes's quiet voice carries an edge of steel. "Not anymore. Neither of them can."

I shake my head, memories pressing in like shadows. "You don't know him. What he's capable of—"

"We know enough." Rhett stands, his movement slow but purposeful. "And we're not letting you face this alone. Not again."

The mist swirls around my feet, responding to the storm of emotions I can't contain. I pull my legs closer, trying to hide the ethereal tendrils from view. Just one more thing they can't know about. One more reason they'd think I'm crazy.

"I should go," I whisper, but even I can hear how hollow the words sound.

"No." Five voices, one word. United in a way that makes my chest ache.

"You're staying," Rhett says firmly. "We're not asking."

"This isn't your problem to fix," I try, but Jace cuts me off.

"Family isn't a problem to fix," he says, all his usual humor stripped away. "It's just what we are. What we've always been."

The truth of his words settles over me like the blankets they've wrapped me in—heavy, suffocating. The mist drifts closer, and I force myself not to look at it, not to acknowledge its presence. They already know too many of my secrets.

My father's voice echoes in my head: *No one wants damaged goods, Bree.*

I close my eyes against the weight of their concern, their determination to help. They don't understand. No matter how many walls they build around me, the darkness always finds its way in.

# Chapter 17
## BREE

My fingers shake as I dial the nursing home's number. Each ring echoes in my ears, mixing with the morning sounds drifting up from the kitchen below—the quiet murmur of voices, the clink of coffee mugs, the illusion of normalcy.

"Maple Grove, this is Sarah."

My throat tightens at her familiar voice. "Sarah, it's Bree. I—" The words stick as Mrs. Henderson's face flashes through my mind. Empty bed. Empty room. Empty—

"Bree?" Sarah's voice softens. "We weren't expecting… honey, take some time. After what happened with Mrs. Henderson—"

"I can work," I cut in. "I just need to change shifts, or—"

"No." The firmness in her tone surprises me. "Take the week. At least. We've got you covered."

My chest tightens. "I can't afford—"

"It's bereavement leave. Paid." Her voice gentles again. "Mrs. H had you listed as next of kin, you know. For notifications."

The phone slips in my sweaty grip. "She what?"

"She changed it months ago. Said you were the only one who really saw her." Sarah pauses. "Take the time, Bree. Please."

The call ends before I can argue. I stare at the phone, Mrs. Henderson's words echoing in my head. *You remind me of my daughter.*

A soft knock breaks through the memory. "Breakfast," Theo calls through the door. "If you're up for it."

My stomach churns at the thought of food, of facing them all again. But hiding won't make this easier.

The kitchen falls quiet when I appear in the doorway. Gray stands by the counter in his work clothes, grease already staining his hands. Wes leans against the far wall, dark eyes steady but unreadable. Theo's laptop glows from his spot at the table, while Rhett watches me over his coffee mug with barely concealed concern.

Jace, predictably, breaks the silence. "There's our sleeping beauty!" He grins, but it doesn't quite reach his eyes. "Coffee? Toast? Small island nation?"

"I should go to work," I mutter, but five different expressions of "no" cut me off.

"Already called Sarah," Gray says, his tone leaving no room for argument. "You're taking time."

Heat crawls up my neck. "You had no right—"

"Bree." Wes's quiet voice somehow carries more weight than Gray's firmness. "Stop."

I wrap my arms around myself, hating how small I feel. How weak. The mist drifts at my feet, and I shift back, praying they don't notice.

"I've got a showing at ten," Jace says, changing the subject with practiced ease. "I'll swing by your place after, grab whatever you need. Handle the lease."

"You don't have to—"

"And!" He continues like I haven't spoken, "Tomorrow night, we feast. I'm thinking lasagna. Garlic bread. Maybe that tiramisu recipe I've been wanting to try."

Rhett snorts. "Last time you tried Italian, the fire department—"

"That was one time," Jace protests. "And technically, the sauce wasn't on fire. It was... aggressively caramelizing."

A laugh bubbles up before I can stop it, small and rusty. Jace's grin softens into something real.

"I have to get back to the garage," Gray says, but he doesn't move. His eyes scan me like he's memorizing details, looking for cracks.

"Go," Theo says without looking up from his laptop. "We've got this."

The weight of those words—*we've got this*—presses against my chest. They don't understand. My father has spent years building his network, making connections. Phil was just the start. There will be others. There always are.

*I should have known better.*

"Here." Rhett pushes a mug of coffee toward me, the gesture achingly familiar. "You look like you need it."

I take it automatically, our fingers brushing. The contact sends a jolt through me, and I step back too quickly. Coffee sloshes over the rim, scalding my hand.

"Shit," I hiss, setting the mug down. "Sorry, I—"

"Don't." Wes appears with a damp cloth, offering it without touching me. "No apologies. Not for this."

I press the cool cloth to my skin, focusing on the sting rather than the knowing look in his eyes. Rather than the way Rhett's hands hover, wanting to help but unsure how.

"Right!" Jace claps his hands, making me jump. "Dinner tomorrow. No arguments. And I'll handle the apartment stuff today." His voice softens slightly. "Unless... you want to come with?"

The thought of going back there—of seeing Phil, of facing my empty apartment—makes my legs weak. "No," I whisper. "I can't."

"Okay." He accepts it easily, like my weakness is nothing to be ashamed of. "I was thinking of stopping by Target after the showing. Could pick up whatever you need." His voice stays deliberately casual. "Clothes, toiletries. Maybe some stuff to make your room feel more like home? There's this fuzzy blanket I saw the other day that screamed 'Bree.'"

*Your room.* The words hit hard, maybe harder than I'd like to admit because that isn't my room. This isn't my home. This is temporary, fragile, bound to shatter the moment they realize how broken I really am.

My father's voice whispers in my head: *They'll see, princess. They'll see what you really are.*

The mist thickens around my ankles, and I step back, needing space, air, anything. "I can't spend the day in your clothes," I say to Rhett, plucking at the borrowed shirt. "Is it okay if I use your washer?"

"Sure," Jace answers before Rhett can. "But seriously, let me grab some stuff for you. Basics, obviously." He pulls out his phone, already making notes. "And that vintage store on Fifth has these cool reading lamps—"

"Jace." My voice cracks. "Stop. Please."

He looks up, his usual grin fading into something more serious. "Too much?"

I wrap my arms around myself, hating how small I feel. How weak. "I can't let you—"

"You can," Wes cuts in, his quiet voice brooking no argument. "And you will."

I flee before anyone can say more, their concern following me up the stairs like a shadow. In the safety of the guest room, I press my forehead against the cool wall.

They think they can fix this. Fix me.

They don't understand that some things stay broken.

# Chapter 18
## JACE

The showing goes about as well as you'd expect when your mind is stuck on old journals and scattered daisies. I smile through the walk-through on autopilot, pointing out crown molding and original hardwood floors while part of me catalogs everything Bree needs. *Clothes. Toiletries. Something to make that room feel less like a guest space and more like home.*

My clients are a young couple, all starry-eyed about their first house. They don't notice how my chatter about the updated kitchen feels hollow, or how my hands shake slightly when I pull out my keys to lock up.

I sit in my car afterward, staring at the Target list on my phone. The practical stuff is easy - basic clothes, shampoo, toothbrush. But it's the other things that matter more. The soft blanket I saw last week that made me think of her. A reading lamp for late nights. Little pieces of comfort she'd never buy for herself.

*Things she couldn't afford to buy for herself.*

The steering wheel creaks under my grip as I think about her apartment. About what waits there. Not just the sparse furniture and empty room, but the ghosts of everything she's been hiding.

My phone buzzes, Theo's name lighting up the screen. My stomach drops - he was supposed to be keeping an eye on her while the rest of us handled damage control.

"What's wrong?" I answer, already turning the key in the ignition.

"Nothing. Well, something." Theo's voice has that tone he gets when he's trying to puzzle something out. "She's in the attic."

I pause, hand hovering over the gear shift. "The attic? How did she even—"

"Found the door unlocked when I went to check on her. She's asleep up there, curled up right where we were planning to put her reading nook." He pauses. "The mist is...different up there. Thicker. Almost like it's trying to tell us something."

"Don't let her wake up alone," I say, pulling out of the parking lot. The universe has a sick sense of humor sometimes - her finding the one place in the house we've been secretly renovating for her. "I'll grab her stuff and be back as soon as I can."

"Jace." Theo's voice stops me before I can hang up. "Be careful at the apartment. Phil might—"

"I know." My free hand tightens on the wheel. "Trust me, part of me hopes he shows up."

"That's exactly why I'm telling you to be careful." Another pause. "The others are still out handling the legal stuff. You'll be alone."

"Good." I end the call before he can argue further, but his warning echoes as I drive. *Be careful.* Like any of us have been careful enough when it comes to Bree.

* * *

The Target bags rustle in my trunk as I pull up to her building. I've probably gone overboard - three throws because I couldn't decide which one she'd like best, a stack of paperbacks from her favorite authors, one of those LED candles that flickers like a real flame. Simple things that might make her stay feel less temporary.

I really hope she likes that green blanket. The soft one that reminded me of her eyes when she actually lets herself smile.

The building looks different today, though not better. Paint peels from the concrete like old scabs, and the front steps are cracked, weeds pushing through like stubborn memories. A cat watches me from a broken windowsill, its yellow eyes following my movement with too much interest.

My key ring feels heavy as I sort through it, finding the spare she'd given us years ago "for emergencies." The one we should have used sooner. Should have walked right in and carried her out of here the first time Phil looked at her wrong.

*Focus, Langston. Get her stuff. Get out. Try not to commit assault if her landlord shows up.*

The lock sticks, just like she said it would. Three jiggles to the left, one sharp turn right. The door groans open like it's warning me about what's inside.

The apartment feels even smaller, emptier somehow. Dust motes dance in the thin sunlight streaming through the window, making the space look almost ethereal—but not in a good way. More like a ghost of what a home should be.

"Jesus, Bree," I mutter, taking in the water stains on the ceiling, the patches of peeling wallpaper. "Why didn't you tell us?"

But I know why. The same reason she never told us about her father. About Phil. About any of it.

I set the empty Target bags by the door and move deeper into the space, cataloging everything with the same attention I usually save for house listings. The couch that's more springs than cushions. The coffee table with cigarette burns that definitely weren't from her. The kitchenette with—I swallow hard—one plate, one mug, like she couldn't even imagine having someone over to share a meal. I open a cabinet, make that two mugs. I can see why she'd never use that one.

I find an old journal peeking out from under the couch, I grab it, careful not to open it. She'd write in this journal for hours when we were kids, hunched over the pages like they could protect her from whatever waited at home. I'd try to make her laugh, tell increasingly ridiculous jokes just to see her smile. Sometimes it even worked.

The mist drifts at my feet, thinner here than at our house but still present.

Movement catches my eye—someone passing by the window. My hands clench automatically, but it's just the cat from earlier, prowling along the ledge. Still, the reminder that Phil could show up any minute gets me moving.

I start with the closet, pulling out the few pieces of clothing she owns. Each item feels like an accusation. *You should have known. Should have seen.* Her uniform from the nursing home. Two pairs of jeans worn soft at the knees. A few bras and panties that she's probably had since high school.

"This is why you never let us visit," I say to the empty room, carefully folding each piece. "Why you always met us somewhere else."

A noise in the hallway makes me freeze, but it's just someone's TV through the thin walls. I force myself to breathe, to focus on the task. *Get her stuff. Get out. Try not to think about how she lived here alone, scared, while we were all comfortable in our big house with our family dinners and movie nights.*

The bathroom's worse. One threadbare towel. Travel-size toiletries like she couldn't afford the regular ones. A crack in the mirror that spiderwebs across the glass, distorting everything it reflects.

I'm taping up the second box on the bathroom floor when I hear it—heavy footsteps in the hall, the distinctive shuffle-stumble of someone who's been drinking. My whole body goes still, listening. The footsteps pause outside her door.

The mist swirls faster around my ankles, agitated. Warning.

*Come on, Phil. Give me a reason.*

A glint catches my eye as I'm checking the medicine cabinet—something metallic behind the mirror's cracked frame. At first I think it's just wiring, but then I notice the lens.

My stomach drops as I reach up, fingers finding the tiny camera expertly hidden in the frame. The kind you wouldn't notice unless you were looking for it. Unless you knew what to look for.

For a moment, I just stare at it, my whole body going cold then hot. The implications hit me like a physical blow—how long it's been here, what it's recorded, whether there are others. Phil's leering face flashes through my mind, his words about watching her.

Bile rises in my throat.

My hand shakes as I pull out my phone, forcing myself to document the camera's placement before carefully removing it. Evidence. We'll need evidence. But God, what I really want to do is find Phil and—

Those heavy footsteps pause outside the door again. A key scrapes in the lock.

The mist churns around my feet, dark and agitated. Waiting.

Every protective instinct I have screams for blood, but Theo's warning echoes in my head. *Be careful.* We need to handle this right. For Bree.

I slip the camera into my pocket, evidence of one more violation she never deserved. One more secret I'll have to tell the others, knowing it will break her heart when she finds out.

*Focus, Langston. Get her stuff out first. Justice comes later.*

I move silently toward the bathroom door, my reflection fractured in the broken mirror. The front door creaks open.

"Bree?" Phil's voice carries that fake concern that makes my skin crawl. "Just checking on my favorite tenant..."

My fists clench together as I hear him move through the apartment. I stay perfectly still, barely breathing, listening to his heavy footsteps draw closer to the bathroom.

The mist swirls around my feet, agitated and dark. Something that sounds like glass clinks in the main room—probably him helping himself to whatever he wants, like he has a right to be here. Like this is his space to invade.

"Breeee," he calls again, dragging out her name. "I didn't see you come in, but I thought I heard... movement."

My fingers brush the camera in my pocket. Everything in me screams to confront him, to make him pay for every violation, every moment of fear he's caused her.

He's close now. I can smell the alcohol on him through the partially open door. One more step and—

His phone rings, the sound sharp and sudden in the quiet apartment. Phil curses, fumbling to answer it.

"Yeah?" Phil listens for a moment, then chuckles darkly. "Nah, she's not here Kevin. But one of those guys she hangs around with is... The pretty boy realtor..."

My jaw clenches. Her father. Of course he's still keeping tabs on her, still trying to control her life even from a distance.

"Yeah, exactly. Always trying to play hero." A pause. "Don't worry, everything's under control. She won't get far... I mean, I'll handle the lease termination properly."

The call ends. Phil's footsteps retreat, slow and deliberate, back toward the front door. That slip about not letting her leave sets off every alarm in my head. This isn't just about the apartment anymore.

The front door closes. Loudly. Too loudly.

He's letting me know he's still here. Waiting.

Phil stands just inside the doorway when I step out of the bathroom, his bulk taking up too much space in the tiny studio. Early afternoon light filters through the grimy window, casting strange shadows across the floor. The mist follows me, curling around my feet in agitated swirls.

My eyes catch on the cracked mirror he installed by the door. *Another camera angle. Bastard really did think of everything.*

"Doing a final inspection?" His voice drips with fake concern, masking something uglier. "Making sure our girl left everything in order?"

*Our girl.* The words make me want to punch something. Preferably his face.

"Actually," I keep my voice light, casual, like we're discussing the weather, "I'm here to help Bree move out. You know how it is—heavy lifting, paperwork, all that fun stuff."

"Without notice? That's not very professional." He shifts his weight, trying to look bigger, more intimidating in the cramped space. "There are proper procedures for these things."

I smile, the kind of smile that makes most people take a step back. "Oh, I'm all about proper procedures. Like the housing authority's guidelines on tenant privacy. Their rules about surveillance." I pull the camera from my pocket, holding it up. "Pretty sure they'd be really interested in your... inspection methods."

The mask slips. Just for a second. But it's enough to see the rage underneath, the same cruel edge I sometimes caught in Bree's father's eyes.

"Careful, pretty boy." Phil's voice drops, turns ugly. "You don't want to make enemies here. Some things are bigger than you understand."

"See, that's where you're wrong." I slip the camera back into my pocket, my smile never wavering. "I understand perfectly. I understand that you and her father thought you could keep controlling her. Keep her scared and alone." I take a step closer. "But that ends today."

His hand twitches toward his pocket. Weapon? Phone? Doesn't matter. The mist surges around my feet, and for a moment, the temperature in the room seems to drop.

"You can't protect her forever," he says, something ugly twisting beneath the words. "She belongs—"

"She belongs wherever she chooses." I cut him off, done playing nice. "And she chooses to leave. So either step aside, or I'll help you move."

We stand there, locked in a moment that stretches like wire about to snap. Part of me hopes he'll try something. Gives me an excuse to—

"Everything okay in there?" A new voice calls from the hall. Theo. Because of course he didn't listen when I said I'd handle it.

Phil's face twists, calculations running behind his bloodshot eyes. After a long moment, he steps back, raising his hands in mock surrender.

Just trying to be helpful," he says with a smile that doesn't reach his eyes. "Make sure everything's... proper.

"We've got it covered," Theo says coolly, appearing in the doorway. His usual calm looks forced, brittle around the edges.

Phil's gaze darts between us, measuring odds I'm guessing he doesn't like. Finally, he shrugs, trying to look casual and failing.

"Have it your way." He takes another step back. "But tell Bree..." His face shifts into something colder, more calculated. "Tell her daddy says hi."

The mist surges, and this time I swear the temperature actually drops. But before either of us can react, Phil turns and walks away, his uneven footsteps echoing down the hall.

"You okay?" Theo asks quietly once he's gone.

I realize my hands are shaking. With rage or adrenaline, I'm not sure. "Found something," I say, pulling out the camera. "And I'm betting it's not the only one."

Theo's expression hardens as he examines it. "We'll have the police—"

"No." I grab another box, needing to move, to do something. "Not yet. This is evidence, yeah, but we handle it smart. For Bree."

He nods, understanding all the things I'm not saying. We pack in silence after that, both of us cataloging every violation, every sign of control we should have seen sooner.

The mist stays with us, watchful and waiting, like it knows this isn't over.

# Chapter 19
## UNKNOWN

The plan unfolds at last. Not as I imagined, but perhaps better. These mortals, her chosen guardians, finally seeing what I've known all along.

*About damn time.*

# Chapter 20
## BREE

I wake to filtered sunlight and the musty scent of old wood. For a moment, I can't place where I am—not my apartment, not the guest room. Dust motes dance in slanted beams that cut through dormer windows, catching on exposed beams overhead.

The attic. I'd found the door earlier when the walls of the guest room started pressing in too close. Needed somewhere higher, somewhere I could breathe. I hadn't expected to find... this.

I shift slightly, realizing I'm curled up in a window seat, soft cushions cradling me. A throw blanket has been tucked around my shoulders, the fabric impossibly soft against my skin.

The mist drifts lazily near the floor, peaceful in a way I've rarely seen it. Like it belongs here. Like maybe I do too.

Nope. I can't let myself think like that.

"You found it." Wes's quiet voice carries from somewhere to my left. I turn my head to see him settled cross-legged on the floor, his back against a bookshelf. "We were wondering when you would."

I blink, taking in the space for the first time in full light. It's been transformed into something out of a dream. Refinished floors gleam beneath oriental rugs. String lights wind through the rafters. The window seat I'm curled in looks custom-built, complete with storage drawers underneath.

"What is all this?" My voice comes out rough with sleep and wonder.

Wes doesn't answer immediately, just watches me with that steady gaze of his. Beyond him, taking up most of the far wall, stands what has to be the biggest bed I've ever seen. It seems like a strange centerpiece for what otherwise looks like a reading nook, but something about it feels... right. Like it was meant to be here, though I can't explain why.

Custom-made, my mind supplies distantly. Has to be. Normal beds don't come that size.

"We've been working on it for a while," Wes finally says, his voice careful but warm. "It started as just storage space, but..." He shrugs, the movement almost shy. "It felt like it needed to be more... For you."

I run my fingers over the window seat cushions, startled to find the fabric is exactly the soft shade of green I've always loved. "You guys did all this?"

"We all helped. Rhett built the window seat. Gray handled the electrical. Theo designed the layout." His lips quirk slightly. "Jace just kept buying things he said you'd like and hiding them up here."

The lump in my throat threatens to choke me. "Why?"

"You know why." He says it simply, like it's the most obvious thing in the world. Like they haven't just revealed they've created an entire space meant for me without even knowing if I'd stay.

The mist swirls closer, curling around my feet like a contented cat. For once, I don't try to hide it. Wes has always seen it anyway, even when I pretended he didn't.

"I don't deserve—" I start, but he cuts me off.

"Don't." The single word carries enough weight to make me look at him. His dark eyes are intense, unwavering. "Do not finish that sentence. Not up here. This space…" He gestures around us. "This is for the truth. And the truth is, you deserve more than we could ever give you."

I pull my knees closer to my chest, trying to ground myself against the wave of emotion threatening to drown me.

Wes nods toward a door I hadn't noticed, tucked between two exposed beams.

"Bathroom through there," Wes says, nodding toward a door tucked between two exposed beams. "Gray went a little overboard with the renovations."

My legs feel shaky as I stand, the throw blanket slipping to the floor. The mist follows as I move toward the door, like it's as curious as I am about what else they've created.

"Oh." The word escapes in a small gasp as I take in the space. The bathroom is bigger than my entire studio apartment, with a tub that could probably fit… I cut that thought off quickly. Heated floors gleam beneath my feet, and soft light spills from fixtures that look antique but feel modern.

"Walk-in closet through there," Wes says from behind me as I notice another door. "Though Jace keeps complaining it's too small."

Too small. I almost laugh. The closet stretches deeper than seems possible, built-in shelves and hanging space that could hold a lifetime of clothes. More space than I'd ever dream of filling.

But something else draws my attention. Half-hidden behind a rack of empty hangers stands another door, its dark wood stark against the white walls. Unlike the others, this one feels… older. Ancient, almost. Like it existed long before their renovations.

My hand reaches for the handle without conscious thought. It doesn't turn.

"That's the one thing we couldn't figure out," Wes says quietly. "No key we've tried works. Gray even had a locksmith look at it, but…" He shrugs. "It won't budge."

The mist curls around the doorframe, thicker than before, almost eager. My fingers tingle where they touch the handle, and for a moment, I swear I feel something pulse beneath the wood, like a heartbeat.

"Bree?" Wes's voice seems to come from far away.

A symbol catches my eye, carved into the doorframe so faintly I almost miss it. It looks like a knot, but more fluid, the lines seeming to shift the longer I stare at them. Something about it tugs at me, familiar in a way that makes no sense.

My fingers trace the pattern before I can stop myself. The door vibrates beneath my touch, just for a second, and the mist surges around my feet.

"Did you feel that?" I whisper, but when I turn to look at Wes, his expression is curious but calm.

"Feel what?"

I pull my hand back, trying to shake off the strange sensation. "The door, it… never mind." I glance at the symbol again. "Has that marking always been there?"

He moves closer, studying it. "I've never noticed it before." His dark eyes shift to me, thoughtful. "But then again, you see things the rest of us miss sometimes."

The mist swirls between us, almost… expectant.

Weird.

I step back from the door, suddenly needing distance from whatever just happened. But the movement brings me closer to Wes, and for once, I don't feel the usual urge to retreat.

"This is real, isn't it?" I gesture at the space around us, this room they've created. "You really want me here."

"We've always wanted you here." His voice is quieter than usual, raw with something I'm afraid to name. "I've wanted..." He stops, seeming to catch himself. "We've been hoping you'd find your way home to us."

Home. The word echoes in my chest, stirring something that feels dangerous. Hopeful.

"I keep waiting," I whisper, staring at the mysterious door rather than meeting his eyes. "For this to fall apart. For you all to realize I'm not worth—"

"Stop." The fierceness in his voice makes me look at him. His usual careful composure cracks, showing something deeper underneath. "Do you know how quiet it's been without you? How wrong? Even when you push us away, even when you run, there's this... space. This Bree-shaped hole nothing else can fill."

My chest feels too tight, like my heart might crack open. Without thinking, I reach for his hand.

Wes goes completely still. His fingers curl around mine slowly, carefully, like he's afraid I might spook. And maybe I should. Maybe I should pull away, rebuild those walls I've worked so hard to maintain.

But his hand is warm, solid, real. An anchor in the storm I've been drowning in.

"I'm glad you're here," he says softly, his thumb brushing over my knuckles. "We all are. But selfishly... I'm really glad you're here."

The mist swirls around our joined hands, and for a moment, everything feels... right. Like puzzle pieces clicking into place.

"Wes?" Gray's voice carries up the stairs, followed by his footsteps. "You up there? Have you heard from—"

He appears in the doorway and stops short. His sharp eyes take in the scene - our joined hands, the comfortable closeness that should feel foreign but somehow doesn't. Something flashes across his face, too quick to read, but it's not jealousy. If anything, it looks like... hope.

I start to pull away, but Wes's fingers tighten slightly. Just enough to say I don't have to run. Not this time.

Gray leans against the doorframe, his expression softening as he takes in my reaction to the room. "You found it."

"It's..." My voice trails off, still overwhelmed by what they've created here. What it means.

"Yours," he says simply. "If you want it."

The normalcy of the moment feels strange but good, like finding something precious you never knew you'd lost. But there's tension in Gray's shoulders, a tightness around his eyes that wasn't there before.

"What's wrong?" Wes asks before I can, his hand still steady around mine.

Gray's jaw tightens. "Theo and Jace haven't checked in. They should have been back by now."

Ice slides down my spine as I remember where they went. My apartment. Phil.

"How long?" Wes's voice carries that dangerous edge it gets when he's worried.

"Too long." Gray pushes off from the doorframe, all pretense of casualness gone. "I'm going to check on them."

"I'll come with you," Wes says, but Gray shakes his head.

"Stay with Bree." His eyes meet mine, and there's something fierce in them. "We're not leaving her alone. Not again."

# Chapter 21
## GRAY

The steering wheel creaks under my grip as I take the corner too fast, muscle memory guiding me down streets I've driven a thousand times. My mind catalogs details with mechanical precision: Theo and Jace's last known location. Time elapsed since their check-in. Phil's usual haunts. Probable scenarios, ranked by risk.

I shouldn't have let them go alone.

The thought circles like an accusation as I pull onto Bree's street. The neighborhood feels different now, filtered through everything we've learned. Every shadow holds potential threats. And Theo and Jace are here alone.

The sound of breaking glass cuts through the quiet, sharp and sudden from the direction of her building. My foot hits the gas before I can think, tires squealing against asphalt. *Please, not again. Not like when we were kids, hearing crashes through those thin walls and being too young, too weak to stop it.*

I slam the truck into park, barely registering the crooked angle across two spaces. Movement catches my eye - Jace's car still in its spot, Theo's around the corner. Both empty.

The mist swirls thickly around my ankles as I approach the building, responding to.. I'm not sure what. It's always been there, hovering at the edges of our lives, but lately it feels more... present. More aware.

Another crash echoes from above, followed by muffled voices. My hands clench as I take the stairs two at a time, instinct warring with the need to think this through. To be smart about it, like Theo would.

The hallway stretches long and dim, emergency lights casting strange shadows. Bree's door stands partially open, spilling harsh fluorescent light into the corridor. The air feels strange - heavy with something that makes the hair on my arms stand up.

I pause just outside, listening. The mist coils around my feet, almost expectant.

"—camera footage?" Theo's voice, tight with barely controlled anger.

"Multiple angles." Jace sounds equally strained. "That fucking mirror by the door? The one in the bathroom? Who knows how many others."

Understanding hits like a physical blow. Cameras. Phil was watching her. Recording her. The rage that floods through me is instant and overwhelming, making my vision blur at the edges.

The mist surges, it seems to be feeding off my anger or maybe responding to it. The temperature drops several degrees.

"Gray." Theo appears in the doorway, his usual calm expression cracked around the edges. "We found—"

"I heard." My voice comes out rougher than I mean it to. "Where is he?"

"Gone." Jace emerges behind Theo, holding something small and electronic. "For now. But he was here earlier. Had a real interesting phone call with daddy dearest."

The casualness of his tone doesn't match the darkness in his eyes. I know that look - have seen it in the mirror every time I remember the sounds that used to come through our shared wall.

"Her father's still..." The words stick in my throat.

"Pulling strings?" Jace's smile is sharp enough to cut. "Oh yeah. Seems our friend Phil's been taking orders this whole time."

My fingers itch to hit something. Someone. But violence won't help her now. We need to be smarter than that.

"The cameras," I say, forcing myself to focus on immediate problems. "Evidence?"

Theo nods, already ahead of me. "Documented placement, took photos. But we can't go to the police. Not yet." He runs a hand through his hair, frustrated. "If we spook them too badly..."

"They might try something worse," I finish. The thought sends ice through my veins.

The mist thickens around us, almost solid now. Through the open door, I can see a couple of boxes stacked neatly - her whole life packed away in cardboard. The sight makes my chest ache.

"We need to move fast," Jace says, pocketing the camera. "Get everything out before—"

A door slams somewhere below, followed by heavy footsteps on the stairs. The mist reacts instantly, coiling like smoke before a fire.

"Back entrance," I say quietly, already moving. "Now."

We work in practiced silence, grabbing boxes and bags. The mist follows as we slip out through the service stairs, helping to obscure our movements or maybe just watching. Always watching.

It's not until we're loading the last box that I catch sight of her nursing uniforms, carefully folded. Such a small collection for someone who gives so much. My throat tightens as I think of how many shifts she must have worked in these, caring for others while barely keeping herself afloat. Of the little girl who used to press her palm against our shared wall, tapping out coded messages when she was too scared to sleep.

The bitter irony doesn't escape me - her most precious memories are safe at home now, but these mundane pieces of her life somehow hit just as hard. Each box feels like evidence of everything we missed, every sign we should have seen sooner.

"Gray." Theo's voice pulls me back. "We need to go."

I nod, carefully placing the box in my truck. We can't protect her from the past, but we can damn well make sure she has a better future.

# Chapter 22
## BREE

"You have cardamom?" The words slip out before I can stop them, surprise overriding my usual caution. The spice cabinet in their kitchen is more organized than I expected, full of things I haven't been able to afford in years.

Wes leans against the counter, watching me with that steady gaze of his. "We have everything."

Something in his tone makes me look up. His dark eyes hold mine, and the weight of what he's not saying settles in my chest. *We have everything you need. Everything you want. Just stay.*

I turn back to the cabinet, fingers trailing over glass jars. "I used to..." The words stick, but I force them out. "My mom taught me this curry recipe. Before she..."

"Show us?" Rhett's voice is carefully neutral, like he's afraid of spooking me. He stands in the doorway, sleeves rolled up, looking more uncertain than I've ever seen him.

The mist drifts lazily around my feet, calm in a way that somehow makes the decision easier. "Okay."

They move around me as I gather ingredients, maintaining careful distance while somehow making the kitchen feel less empty. Rhett chops onions with the same precise focus he brings to everything, while Wes measures spices I call out without questioning why I don't need to look up amounts.

"You've done this before," Wes observes quietly when I add spices by feel rather than measuring.

I swallow hard, stirring the onions Rhett hands me. "After mom left… Dad didn't really cook. So I had to learn. Had to remember what she taught me."

The wooden spoon scrapes against the pot, filling the silence that follows. I wait for the questions, the pity, but neither comes. Instead, Wes just slides me the ginger I hadn't even asked for yet.

"Here." His fingers brush mine as he passes the root, and for once, I don't flinch. The touch is so light, so casual, I almost miss it. Almost.

The mist swirls contentedly as I add more spices, the familiar scents filling the kitchen. For a moment, I can almost pretend I'm somewhere else. Someone else. Someone who belongs in this warm kitchen with its well-stocked cabinets and people who look at me like I matter.

"Smells amazing," Rhett says, pausing his chopping to peer into the pot. "You said your mom taught you?"

"Yeah…" I stir faster, focusing on the movement. "She said cooking was like magic. Taking simple things and making them into something better." *Something worth keeping*, I don't add. *Something worth loving.*

"She was right." Wes's voice is closer than I expect. He stands near my shoulder, not quite touching but present. "About the magic part."

I glance up to find him watching me with an expression I can't quite read. The mist curls around both our feet, and for a second, I swear I feel… something. Like static electricity but warmer.

"Shit," Rhett mutters behind us, breaking the moment. "Sorry, I think I murdered this tomato."

A laugh bubbles up before I can stop it. The sound surprises me - rusty but real.

"Here." I move to his cutting board, gesturing at the mangled vegetable. "Like this." I demonstrate with another tomato, my movements sure despite years of disuse.

Rhett watches intently, standing close enough that I can feel his warmth. "You're good at this," he says softly. "Really good."

"I..." The praise catches me off guard. "It's just practice."

"It's more than that." Wes appears on my other side, handing me more tomatoes. "You know exactly what you're doing. Like you've got some sixth sense about flavors."

I duck my head, uncomfortable with the attention but not... not hating it. "The rice needs to start soon," I mumble, deflecting. "If we want everything ready at the same time."

They let me change the subject, but I feel their eyes on me as I move through the kitchen. It should make me nervous, being watched. But something about their presence feels... steady. Safe.

The curry comes together like I remember, rich and fragrant. I add a final pinch of garam masala, and the scent hits me hard - memory wrapped in spice and steam. Mom in our tiny kitchen, laughing as she taught me to bloom spices. Her hand over mine on the spoon, showing me how to stir without splashing.

"Bree?" Wes's voice is gentle. When I look up, I realize I've stopped stirring, lost in the memory.

"Sorry, I..." I blink hard against the sudden sting in my eyes. "It just... it smells like home. Like it used to be."

Rhett moves like he wants to reach for me but stops himself. "Thank you," he says instead. "For sharing this with us."

The words feel bigger than they should, heavy with meaning I'm not ready to examine. I focus on plating the food instead, falling back on movements that don't require thought.

The front door opens, voices drifting up from the entryway. Gray's low rumble, Theo's measured tone, Jace trying too hard to sound normal. Something's wrong - I can hear it in the careful way they're speaking, see it in how Wes and Rhett exchange glances.

But when they appear in the kitchen doorway, their faces shift to genuine surprise.

"Holy shit, what smells amazing?" Jace asks, his usual grin sliding into place as he peers at the stove.

"Bree cooked," Rhett says, and there's something like pride in his voice that makes my cheeks warm.

Gray leans against the doorframe, some of the tension leaving his shoulders as he takes in the scene. Theo moves to help set the table, his movements deliberately casual in a way that would worry me if I let myself think about it.

But the mist stays calm, appearing and disappearing between all of us like it's holding something together. And when we sit down to eat, the conversation flows easier than it should, filling the kitchen with a warmth that has nothing to do with curry.

I notice the careful way they avoid certain topics, the looks they think I don't see. But for now, maybe it's enough to just be here, watching Jace dramatically fan his mouth from the spice while Theo rolls his eyes. Feeling Wes's quiet presence beside me as Gray asks for seconds.

Maybe, just for tonight, I can pretend this is normal. That I belong here, in this moment, with them.

The others insist on cleaning up, brushing off my attempts to help. Even Jace, who normally avoids dishes like they might bite him, starts gathering plates.

"Come on," he says, nodding toward the stairs. "Got something to show you."

I hesitate, glancing at the others, but they're already settling into a rhythm - Rhett washing, Wes drying, Theo putting things away while Gray wipes down counters. It should feel strange, how naturally they work together, but something about it just feels... right.

The mist follows as Jace leads me upstairs to the guest room. He's uncharacteristically quiet, missing his usual swagger. When he pushes open the door, I freeze in the doorway.

Bags cover the bed - more than I can count at first glance. Not just Target, but other stores I'd never let myself shop at. A mountain of soft things in shades of green and blue, tags still attached.

"I might have gone a little overboard," Jace says, running a hand through his hair. The gesture makes him look younger, almost nervous. "But I saw this blanket, and it reminded me of your eyes when you actually smile, you know? And then there were these sweaters that seemed warm, and you're always cold, and..." He trails off, watching my face. "Too much?"

I step closer, running my fingers over the nearest item. The fabric is softer than anything I own. "Jace, I..." My throat tightens. "I can't accept all this."

"Sure you can." He bounces on his toes, that restless energy of his returning. "Look, this one's my favorite." He pulls out something impossibly soft and green. "Feel it."

The sweater feels like clouds in my hands. I check the tag before I can stop myself and my knees go weak. "This costs more than I make in two shifts."

"Good." His voice loses its playful edge. "Because you deserve nice things, Bree. Things that feel good. Things that keep you warm." He starts pulling out more items - pajamas, socks, things I haven't been able to replace in years. "And before you argue about money - this is nothing compared to what I spend on my hair products."

A laugh catches in my throat, coming out more like a sob. There's more clothing here than I've owned in my entire adult life. Things picked with obvious care - comfortable but pretty, practical but not cheap. Things chosen by someone who knows me, who sees me.

"I got you some books too," he says softer, gesturing to a stack on the dresser. "The ones you used to read until they fell apart. And this—" He pulls out a small lamp with a dimmer switch. "For late nights when you can't sleep. The light changes colors."

My vision blurs as I sink onto the edge of the bed. The mist curls around my ankles, calm and steady. "Why?" I whisper.

"Because we love you, dummy." He says it easily, like it's the most obvious thing in the world. "And yeah, I know you're not ready to hear that. But tough luck - we're not going anywhere."

I press my face into the soft sweater, breathing in the new-clothes smell, trying to hold back tears. Jace sits beside me, close but not touching.

"You don't have to wear any of it," he says quietly. "We can send it all back if you hate it. But please... please let us do this. Let us help make this feel like home."

A tear escapes despite my best efforts, soaking into the sweater. Jace pretends not to notice, just starts showing me more things - pajamas with little stars on them, fuzzy socks in ridiculous patterns, a robe that feels like being hugged by a cloud.

And somewhere between his dramatic commentary on each item and the gentle way he handles things he picked just for me, I stop trying to fight the tears. Stop trying to pretend this doesn't mean everything.

The mist settles around us like a blanket, peaceful and content, as Jace's steady stream of chatter fills the space where my words can't reach.

For a long moment, I just sit there, surrounded by more kindness than I know how to process. Jace's voice washes over me, a comforting backdrop as I run my fingers over soft fabrics and try to breathe through the tightness in my chest.

"Oh, and check this out," Jace says, reaching for something on the nightstand. "It's one of those white noise machines. You can set it to rain or ocean waves or whatever. Thought it might help with..." He trails off, but I know what he means. The nightmares. The restless nights when sleep feels like a distant memory.

I nod, not trusting my voice. The thoughtfulness of it all threatens to overwhelm me. Each item feels like a piece of armor against the cold, empty life I've been living. A shield against the loneliness that's been my constant companion for so long.

"Jace," I manage finally, my voice barely above a whisper. "I don't know what to say."

He grins, but it's softer than his usual cocky smile. "You don't have to say anything. Just... maybe try some of it on? See how it feels?"

I hesitate, then nod. "Okay. I... I can do that."

"Great!" He bounces to his feet. "I'll give you some privacy. Take your time, okay? And if anything doesn't fit or you don't like it, we can exchange it. No pressure."

He's almost to the door when I find my voice again. "Jace?"

He turns, eyebrows raised in question.

"Thank you," I say softly. "For... for seeing me."

Something flashes across his face - too quick for me to name, but it makes my chest ache. "Always, Bree," he says, his voice uncharacteristically serious. "We see you. All of us do."

Then he's gone, closing the door gently behind him. I'm left alone with a mountain of gifts and a lump in my throat that won't seem to fade.

The mist swirls around my ankles as I stand, drifting over the piles of clothing like it's exploring too. I reach for the green sweater first, the one that reminded Jace of my eyes. It slips over my head like a cloud, impossibly soft against my skin.

I catch a glimpse of myself in the mirror and freeze. The girl staring back at me looks... different. Softer somehow, less sharp around the edges. The sweater brings out flecks of gold in my eyes I've never noticed before.

For a moment, I can almost see what they see when they look at me. Someone worth protecting. Someone worth loving.

# Chapter 23
## WES

The kitchen is too quiet. Not the kind of peaceful quiet that settles over a late-night meal or a good conversation. This is heavy, choking. The kind of silence that presses on your chest and makes your pulse tick louder in your ears.

I lean against the counter, staring at the shadowy yard through the window. The faint reflection of the kitchen catches my eye—Gray leaning against the fridge, arms crossed like he's trying to hold himself together. Theo is perched on the edge of a chair, his head bowed, fingers laced tightly as if in prayer. Rhett sits at the table, his jaw set so tight I'm half-waiting for his teeth to crack.

No one says a damn thing. No one has to.

The sound of footsteps on the stairs cuts through the quiet. Jace steps into the room, his usual lightness gone. His hair's a mess, shirt wrinkled, and for the first time I can remember, he doesn't meet any of our eyes. Just stares at some point on the floor between us.

"She's asleep," he says finally, his voice carrying none of its usual warmth. "Took a while, but...finally."

Rhett's shoulders ease, just barely, and Theo nods like the news is a lifeline we've all been holding out for.

"She okay?" I ask, though I already know the answer.

Jace shrugs, not meeting our eyes. "As okay as she can be. She crashed hard. Looked like she'd been running on fumes for weeks. Didn't say much."

I glance over at Rhett, whose fingers drum against the table. He doesn't look up, doesn't say anything, but the tension in his frame says it all.

"We need to talk," Jace says after a beat, looking at each of us in turn. "And not here."

Gray straightens. "Why not?"

"Because if she overhears this..." Jace trails off, running a hand through his hair. "It's gonna shake her. Bad."

"Attic," Theo suggests, already standing. "It's the quietest place in the house."

Rhett's head snaps toward him. "The attic?"

"She found it today," Theo says, his voice measured but with an edge of something. "I didn't mention it because I didn't really have time. But I found her sleeping up there earlier."

Rhett stiffens. "And you didn't tell me?"

Theo doesn't flinch under the weight of Rhett's glare. "Today's been a little crazy"

I push off the counter, interrupting before this turns into something. "He's right. The attic's the best place for this. She won't hear us up there."

Gray nods reluctantly, pushing off the fridge. "Let's go."

We climb the stairs in near silence, the weight of unspoken things trailing behind us. The attic door creaks open, and I'm hit by a strange sense of familiarity. The space is clean, mostly finished, but there's a faint scent hanging in the air that's unmistakable. Bree.

The light filtering through the window catches on mismatched furniture—pieces we've been bringing up here bit by bit, waiting for the day she'd let us finish this for her. The walls are painted soft gray, the kind of color she always picked when we helped her redecorate as kids. The big window seat is there too, the one she found earlier.

Gray shuts the door behind us, leaning against it like he's trying to hold back the weight of the world. "All right," he says, his tone sharp. "Out with it."

Theo pulls something small and black from his pocket and places it on the desk. Jace follows suit, setting another identical object beside it.

Cameras.

My blood goes cold. "What the hell are those?"

"Cameras," Theo says flatly. "We found them in her apartment. Hidden in the mirrors, above the door, maybe more we didn't catch."

The words don't register at first. Or maybe I just don't want them to. "You're saying he was watching her?"

"Not just him," Jace mutters, leaning against the desk. His easy demeanor is gone, replaced by something darker. "Her dad too. Phil got a call from him while I was there. Sounded like they've been working together."

The room drops a few degrees. Or maybe that's just me. My pulse pounds in my ears, anger and protectiveness surging so fast I feel like I might snap. I grip the back of the chair to steady myself, trying to keep the fire under control.

"Phil," Rhett growls, his voice low and dangerous. "Her father."

Jace nods, his expression grim. "Phil was planted. Her dad's been pulling strings for years, keeping her isolated, keeping her broken."

Rhett slams his fist against the wall, the sound sharp and final. "And we didn't see it."

"Fuck man, stop. Bree doesn't need to see that." Gray says, already inspecting the new dent in the wall.

"No one saw what was going on." Theo says, his tone steady but his jaw tight. "But now we know. And now we act."

"Act?" I echo, my voice rough. "We should've acted years ago. We should've—"

"We didn't know," Gray cuts in, his voice cutting through my spiraling thoughts. "And beating ourselves up now doesn't help her."

"Doesn't it?" I snap, my voice sharper than I meant it to be. "Because I can't stop thinking about all the times we were right there and didn't—"

"We know." Gray's voice is quieter now, but it carries more weight. "We all know."

The mist curls around my feet, cold and steady, like it's trying to anchor me. Or maybe it's feeding off the fury swirling in the room. Either way, I force myself to breathe. To think. Because this isn't about my anger or my guilt. This is about Bree.

Jace picks up one of the cameras, turning it over in his hand. "We've got evidence now. And we've got a plan."

"What plan?" Rhett asks, his green eyes blazing.

Jace glances at Theo, who nods. "We deal with Phil. Quietly, for now. Make sure Bree doesn't have to see him again. And we figure out what to do about her dad."

"Her dad." Rhett spits the words like a curse. "He's still out there. Still—"

"And we'll deal with him too," Gray interrupts, his voice hard. "But one step at a time. Right now, Bree doesn't know about the cameras or the call. If she finds out…"

"She won't," I say firmly, the promise burning in my chest. "Not yet. Not until she's ready."

The silence that follows feels heavy but unified. We don't have all the answers, but we'll get them for her.

# Chapter 24
## BREE

Dawn filters through unfamiliar curtains, painting shadows I don't recognize on walls that still feel strange. The guest room is quiet without the usual sounds of my apartment building creaking and groaning around me. No arguments filtering through paper-thin walls. No footsteps overhead that make my heart race.

Just silence. And the mist, curling lazily at the edges of my vision like it always does when I wake.

Sleep isn't coming back. I know that feeling too well. The restlessness that creeps in when everything is too still, too peaceful. When you're waiting for the other shoe to drop.

My feet hit the cool hardwood as I slide out of bed. Rhett's borrowed t-shirt falls to my thighs, and I tug it lower, hyperaware of the scars on my legs. Even here, even alone, the instinct to hide runs deep.

The mist follows as I slip into the hallway, drawn upward like it knows where I'm going before I do. The attic door stands partly open, early light spilling down the stairs. I don't remember leaving it that way.

The attic feels different in the dawn light. Softer somehow. I drift toward the window seat that caught my attention yesterday, running my fingers over fabric that's exactly the shade of green I've always loved. The mist swirls contentedly around my feet as I settle onto the cushions, drawing my knees to my chest.

From here, I can see the whole backyard, still misty in the early light. The guys have strung lights through the old oak tree, and they sway gently in the morning breeze, unlit but somehow still magical. Like this whole space - this whole house - exists in some parallel universe where broken things can be beautiful.

I don't hear him come up the stairs. Don't realize I'm not alone until his voice breaks through my thoughts, low and careful.

"You're beautiful like this."

I startle, turning to find Wes in the doorway. Heat floods my cheeks as I tug at Rhett's shirt, suddenly too aware of how much of me is exposed. But Wes's dark eyes hold mine, steady and sure, like he's seeing straight through all my defenses.

"Don't," I whisper, though I'm not sure if I'm talking to him or myself.

He moves closer, his steps measured like he's approaching a spooked animal. "Don't what? Tell you the truth?"

The mist curls between us, and I swear the temperature shifts slightly. Not cold, but... different. Like the air itself is holding its breath.

"I'm not—" I start, but he cuts me off.

"You are." His voice is quiet but firm. "Sitting here in the morning light, finally letting yourself rest. Finally letting us..." He trails off, and something in his expression makes my chest ache. "You're the most beautiful thing I've ever seen."

The words do something to my insides, and I have to look away. Back to the window, the yard, anything but the raw honesty in his eyes. Because he means it. And that terrifies me more than any threat ever could.

The silence stretches between us, delicate as spun glass. I expect him to leave - to let me retreat behind my walls like everyone always does. But instead, he moves to sit beside me, leaving careful space between us.

"You know," he says after a moment, his voice softer than I've ever heard it, "I remember the first time I saw you. Really saw you."

I turn slightly, caught off guard by the vulnerability in his tone. Wes doesn't do this - doesn't open up, doesn't share. But here he is, staring out at the misty yard like he's seeing something else entirely.

"We were what, eight? Nine? You were sitting on the front steps of the complex, reading some book that was way too big for you." A ghost of a smile touches his lips. "The sun caught your hair just right, and you had this little wrinkle between your eyebrows because you were concentrating so hard."

The memory hits me unexpectedly - a warm afternoon, the weight of my mother's old copy of The Secret Garden in my lap. "I remember that book. The cover was falling off."

"But you treated it like it was precious." He glances at me, and there's something in his dark eyes that makes my breath catch. "That's when I knew."

"Knew what?" My voice comes out barely above a whisper.

"That you were going to matter. That you already did." He looks down at his hands, and I realize they're trembling slightly. "You've always been beautiful, Bree. Even when you're trying your hardest not to be seen. Maybe especially then."

The mist swirls around us both now, and I swear it feels warmer, like it's trying to hold this moment still. Keep it safe.

"Wes," I start, but I don't know how to finish. How to handle this glimpse behind his carefully maintained control. This gift of vulnerability he's offering.

The weight of his words settles in my chest, making it hard to breathe. Because this is Wes - quiet, steady Wes who watches everything but shares nothing. Wes who's always been there, a shadow at the edges of every memory, seeing more than any of us realized.

"I used to watch you read," he continues, his voice low like he's sharing secrets. "You'd get lost in those books for hours. It was the only time you ever looked... peaceful." He pauses, and I catch the slight clench of his jaw. "The only time you weren't flinching at shadows."

My throat tightens. "You noticed that?"

"I noticed everything." His hands flex against his thighs, and I realize how much this is costing him - this sharing, this openness. "The way you'd check every room before entering. How you never sat with your back to a door. The times you'd disappear for days, then come back with sleeves pulled down over your arms."

The mist thickens around us, responding to the surge of emotion I'm trying desperately to contain. I should feel exposed, raw. But something about his quiet confession makes me brave enough to whisper, "Why didn't you say anything?"

His eyes meet mine, dark and intense. "Because you weren't ready. Because pushing you would have meant losing you completely." His voice roughens slightly. "And I couldn't— we couldn't lose you."

The space between us feels charged, heavy with years of unspoken things. With all the times he saw me, really saw me, and chose to wait. To stay. To watch over me from a distance because it was all I could handle.

"I'm still broken," I whisper, the words slipping out before I can stop them.

"No." The fierceness in his voice makes me look at him. "You're surviving. You're fighting. And you're letting us in, even though it terrifies you." His hand moves, hovering near mine on the window seat cushion. Not touching, but close enough that I can feel his warmth. "That's not broken, Bree. That's brave."

The weight of his words settles over me like the mist curling around our feet, warm and grounding in a way I'm not used to. Wes doesn't push, doesn't demand more than I can give, but his presence is a steady anchor in the storm of my thoughts.

I should say something. Anything. But my throat tightens, the words tangling before they can form. Instead, I do the only thing I can think of—the only thing that feels right.

I lean forward, resting my head against his shoulder.

Wes stiffens for a fraction of a second before he exhales, the tension bleeding out of him. His warmth seeps into me, his steady presence chasing away the cold I didn't realize I'd been holding onto.

Neither of us speaks. We just sit there, the quiet stretching between us, heavy with everything that's been left unsaid—and yet, somehow, it feels like enough. His shoulder is solid beneath me, his scent—citrus and cedar—calming the edges of my frayed nerves.

The mist swirls thicker now, curling around us like it's watching. Protecting. Approving.

For the first time in a long time, I feel... safe.

And I let myself stay. Just for a little while.

* * *

Wes gave me some space, slipping out of the attic with a lingering glance that said more than words could. I stayed by the window, watching the mist dance around my feet as the sun rose higher, warming the pale gray walls. But the quiet that had felt so comfortable with him here now pressed in, making my thoughts spiral.

*What am I doing? Letting my guard down, letting them see me like this...*

I pace the length of the attic, my bare feet silent against the wooden floors. The mist follows, thicker than usual, almost urgent in the way it curls around my ankles. Like it's trying to tell me something.

The space feels different now, bathed in the soft light of late morning. Warmer, somehow.

The mark catches my eye immediately - sharper than before, its edges seeming to shimmer in the late morning light. It's not quite a symbol, not quite writing, but something in between. The lines flow like water frozen mid-stream, forming what might be a crown, or maybe a knot. The longer I stare, the more it seems to move, though I know that's impossible.

My fingers brush the wood before I can stop myself. The mark feels warm beneath my touch, humming with something that makes my skin tingle.

The mist swirls higher as I crouch down, drawn by something on the floor beneath the doorframe. At first, it just looks like dirt, scattered in a small, neat pile. But when I reach out, the texture is different—softer, finer.

Seeds.

I scoop them into my hand, letting them sift through my fingers. They're tiny, dark, and unremarkable, but something about them feels... significant. Like they're meant for me. They're unlike any seeds I've seen before - dark as night but with a faint iridescent sheen, like oil on water. They feel impossibly light in my palm, almost weightless, yet there's a weight to them that has nothing to do with their size. Something about them reminds me of the daisies that used to appear on my windowsill, though I couldn't say why.

The urge to plant them comes out of nowhere, sharp and insistent. It's ridiculous—I don't know the first thing about gardening, and I've never been one for getting my hands dirty. But the idea takes root, and before I know it, I'm heading downstairs, the seeds clutched tightly in my palm.

The backyard is cool and damp from the morning rain, the earth soft beneath my bare feet. The mist lingers in the corners of the yard, curling around the edges of the old oak tree where the guys strung up the lights. It feels like it's watching, waiting to see what I'll do.

I kneel near the base of the tree, the damp grass soaking through Rhett's borrowed sweatpants. My fingers dig into the soil, hesitant at first, then with more purpose. The earth smells rich and alive, and for the first time in what feels like forever, I don't feel weighed down by the ghosts of my past.

The seeds slip from my hand into the shallow holes I've made, and I cover them gently, pressing the soil down with care. It's a small act, almost meaningless, but something inside me shifts as I sit back on my heels, wiping my hands on my pants.

The mist swirls closer, wrapping around the base of the tree and then winding its way up into the branches. The air feels warmer, lighter, like it's responding to the simple act of planting something, of starting fresh.

For a moment, I just sit there, letting the quiet settle over me. The weight in my chest feels a little less heavy, the shadows in my mind a little less dark.

# Chapter 25
## THEO

The coffee maker hums, a steady counterpoint to my racing thoughts as I watch Bree through the kitchen window. She looks small against the backdrop of the old oak tree, knees pressed into damp earth, morning light catching on her dark hair. Her borrowed clothes - Rhett's sweatpants, my hoodie - make her seem both more fragile and more *here* than she's been in years.

I've seen her run. Hide. Fight. But I've never seen her like this - on her knees in our backyard, fingers buried in soil like she's searching for something. The mist curls around her in ways I've never witnessed before, almost protective in its intensity.

"That's new."

I don't startle at Gray's voice behind me - we're all moving carefully these days, making our presence known before we get too close. Old habits from watching Bree flinch at sudden sounds.

"The gardening or the mist?" I ask, though I know the answer. Gray's probably been cataloging the mist's changing behavior as carefully as I have.

He moves to stand beside me, his own coffee forgotten in his hand. There's tension in his jaw that wasn't there yesterday, before we found the cameras. Before we knew just how deep this went.

"Both." His voice carries that edge it gets when he's trying to solve a problem he can't fix with his hands. "She was in the attic again this morning."

"With Wes," I add, remembering the quiet way Wes came down earlier, something raw and careful in his expression. "I heard them talking."

"She let him close," Gray says, and there's something like hope beneath his measured tone. "Didn't pull away."

I nod, watching as Bree sits back on her heels, studying whatever she's planted with an intensity I haven't seen since we were kids and she'd lose herself in books. The mist weaves through the tree branches above her, casting strange shadows that seem to move independently of the breeze.

"We need to tell her." The words taste bitter, but necessary. "About the cameras. About Phil and her father—"

"Not yet." Gray's hand tightens around his mug. "She's just starting to..." He trails off, watching as Bree presses her palm flat against the earth, the mist swirling thicker around her. "Did you notice the mark on that door upstairs?"

The change of subject isn't subtle, but I let it slide. "Yeah. It wasn't there until she went up there."

"You sure about that?"

I glance at him, catching the sharp edge in his tone. "What do you mean?"

"I mean," Gray says carefully, "a lot of things are changing. The mist. The door. Her." He sets his mug down, bracing his hands against the counter. "We've been watching that mist follow her around since we were kids, pretending it was normal. But this feels different."

Through the window, Bree stands, brushing dirt from her knees. The mist follows her movement, and for a moment, it almost looks like it's reaching for her.

"Jace said Phil saw something," I say quietly. "Right before he backed off. Something in the mist that scared him."

Gray's jaw tightens. "Yeah. Well, he's going to see a lot worse if he comes near her again."

"That's not what I meant." I turn to face Gray fully, noting the shadows under his eyes, the tension in his shoulders. We're all carrying the weight of what we found, but Gray's taking it harder. Maybe because he lived closest to her back then, heard things through those thin walls that still haunt him. "The mist is responding to her differently. Like it's... awakening."

Through the window, Bree crouches again, reaching for something near the base of the oak. The mist coils around her outstretched hand, and I swear I see it pulse, just for a moment.

"Like that door upstairs," Gray says, following my gaze. "The way it reacts when she's near it."

I remember Wes telling me about her tracing that strange symbol yesterday, how the air seemed to thicken, how the mist surged around her feet. "She sees things we don't," I say carefully. "Always has."

"And we pretended not to notice." Gray's voice carries an edge of self-recrimination. "Just like we pretended not to see other things."

"We were kids," I remind him, though the words feel hollow. "We didn't understand—"

"We're not kids anymore." He pushes off from the counter, running a hand through his hair. "And we can't keep pretending this is normal. The cameras, her father, the mist... it's all connected somehow."

I think about the footage Jace described, the careful documentation of Bree's private moments. The way Phil's hands shook when he talked about her father's plans. "You think her father knows? About the mist?"

"I think he knows something." Gray's eyes narrow as Bree stands again, this time holding something small and green. A seedling, maybe. "Why else keep such close tabs on her? Why plant Phil to watch her?"

"Maybe he's just a sick fuck who wants to rape his daughter again," I say, the words tasting like ash in my mouth. The coffee maker's cheerful beep feels obscene against the weight of that truth.

Gray flinches, but doesn't argue. We both know the depths of Bree's father's depravity. The cameras were just the latest violation in a long history of abuse.

"We need a plan," I say, reaching for new mugs on autopilot. "If her father's been watching this whole time, he's not going to just let her go."

"No," Gray agrees, his voice dropping. "But he's never dealt with all of us before. Not really."

I pour coffee, letting the familiar ritual steady my hands. "Rhett wants to confront him directly."

"Rhett wants to burn the world down." Gray accepts the mug I offer, his knuckles white around the ceramic. "But that's not what she needs right now."

"What does she need?"

"Time." He watches as Bree moves to another spot beneath the oak, the mist following like a loyal pet. "Space to heal. To trust again." His jaw tightens. "To figure out whatever's happening with the mist without her father's shadow hanging over her."

I think about the changes we've seen in just the past few days. How she's slowly letting her guard down, allowing small touches, accepting help. The way the mist grows stronger, more purposeful, as she does.

"She's going to find out eventually," I say quietly. "About the cameras. About all of it."

"I know." Gray sets his mug down with careful precision. "But right now, she needs to feel safe. To know she has a home here, with us." He pauses, something flickering across his expression. "That curry last night... I've known her my whole life and never even knew she could cook like that."

I nod, remembering how her quiet pride had shown through when we all sat down to eat, the way she watched us from beneath her lashes as we tasted it. "Her mother taught her before she left." The words feel weighted with everything we're learning about her, all these hidden parts she's kept locked away.

"That's what she needs," Gray says firmly. "Space to remember who she is without her father's voice in her head. Without fear." His eyes track Bree's movements through the garden, the way she seems more grounded with each careful planting. "The rest... we'll handle the rest."

I watch her through the window, something tightening in my chest. Everyone thinks I'm the analytical one, the one who approaches everything with logic and careful planning. But when it comes to Bree... She looks up suddenly, catching my eye through the glass. For a moment, her lips curve into a small, hesitant smile – the kind that makes my carefully ordered thoughts scatter like leaves in wind. She's always had that effect on me, since we were kids. The way she'd curl up with a book, lost in worlds I wanted to explore with her. How she'd help me with chemistry homework even when she was exhausted, her quiet voice making complex formulas feel like poetry.

The smile fades as she turns back to her planting, but the ache in my chest lingers. Some things can't be solved with logic. Some things just have to be felt, carried, protected. Like the way my heart trips every time she lets down another wall, every time she shares another piece of herself she's kept hidden for so long.

The mist swirls around her fingers as she works, and I swear it pulses in time with my heartbeat.

# Chapter 26
## BREE

The early morning quiet feels different here. It's not the fragile kind of quiet, the kind that hangs in the air waiting to be broken by raised voices or slammed doors. This quiet feels steady, like it's meant to be here. Like it belongs.

I shift under the heavy blanket, Rhett's oversized hoodie still draped over my shoulders. The faint scent of cedar clings to it, grounding me as I sit up and glance around the guest room. Light filters through the curtains, soft and golden, casting warm patterns on the walls. My apartment never looked like this in the morning—never felt like this.

The sound of movement draws me toward the door. A soft clink of a plate, the faint hum of a kettle. My bare feet touch the cool floor as I stand, tugging the hoodie tighter around me. The mist curls lazily at my ankles, a silent companion as I make my way down the hall.

Gray is in the kitchen, moving with quiet efficiency. He's already dressed, his shirt sleeves rolled to the elbows, revealing forearms that move with practiced ease as he slices something on the cutting board. The sight of him—focused, steady, so effortlessly capable—does something to my chest, makes it harder to breathe for a moment. The smell of coffee lingers in the air, mingling with the faint aroma of butter and something warm and earthy. My stomach growls softly, betraying me before I can even announce my presence.

I take a hesitant step closer, my fingers brushing the edge of the counter as I try to make myself small, unnoticed. But my eyes keep straying to him—his forearms flexing as he works, the way his dark hair catches the morning light. He's not even trying, and yet he draws me in. They all do.

It's maddening. It's infuriating. It's... terrifying.

Because I can never let them know. Not about the way my heart stumbles every time Rhett meets my eyes, steady and sure. Or how Wes's quiet strength feels like a tether I didn't realize I needed. Or how Jace's easy charm makes me feel like the world isn't such a heavy place. Or the way Theo's calm steadiness feels like a balm against all the chaos in my head.

And Gray? God, Gray makes it worse. He's all sharp edges and protective instincts, his gaze cutting through every wall I've ever built like they're nothing. The way he looks at me—like I'm something worth figuring out—makes it impossible to forget what I've lost. What I can't allow myself to want.

Being here, surrounded by them, makes it so much harder. I told myself I'd stay for a night, two at most. But every small kindness, every shared look, every moment like this—watching Gray move through the kitchen like it's the most natural thing in the world—it chips away at my resolve. Makes me wonder if maybe, just maybe, I could let myself want this.

But I can't. Not without ruining everything.

He doesn't look up right away, but I know he heard me. Gray hears everything. "Morning," he says, his voice low and calm, like he's speaking into the stillness of the house.

"Morning." My voice is quieter than I intend, but it doesn't feel out of place here. I hover near the edge of the room, unsure if I should stay.

"Coffee's fresh." He gestures toward the pot without turning, his attention still on whatever he's chopping. "Mugs are in the cabinet above."

I nod, stepping into the room and feeling the cool tile under my feet. It feels too... normal, this routine of mornings. Too easy. I grab a mug and pour the coffee, the steam curling upward like the mist that always lingers nearby.

Gray sets down the knife, finally looking over at me. His sharp green eyes soften slightly, but he doesn't push. "You sleep okay?"

The question catches me off guard, even though it shouldn't. "Yeah," I lie. "Better than usual."

His mouth quirks in something that's not quite a smile, but close enough to feel like one. "Good."

We don't say much else as he plates up whatever he was working on—scrambled eggs and toast, simple but comforting. He sets a plate in front of me at the kitchen island without a word, then takes his own seat across from me. The quiet isn't awkward. It just... is.

I watch him as he eats, his movements precise but unhurried. It's a stark contrast to the mornings I've known—rushed, chaotic, or filled with too much noise to enjoy anything. This is something else entirely. It feels steady. Safe.

When I finish, I stand to take my plate to the sink, but something catches my eye outside the window. My breath catches.

The seeds.

They've sprouted.

I set the plate down carefully, stepping closer to the window. The little patch of soil where I planted the seeds yesterday is now dotted with delicate green stems, their leaves already stretching toward the sunlight. A faint shimmer seems to cling to them, like morning dew catching the light just so.

It's impossible. Seeds don't sprout overnight. Not like this.

My heart races, but not with fear. There's something about the sight—about the way they've grown, impossibly fast yet undeniably real—that feels... right. Like they belong here. Like I belong here.

"Bree?"

Gray's voice pulls me back. I turn to find him watching me, his fork paused halfway to his mouth. His gaze flicks from my face to the window, and I know he sees it too.

For a moment, he looks like he's going to say something. But then he doesn't. He just nods slightly, his expression calm but knowing, and goes back to eating like nothing's out of the ordinary.

I glance back at the small buds, the shimmer still faintly visible in the sunlight. The mist curls around my feet, warmer than usual, almost like it's pleased.

And for the first time in a long time, I let myself smile.

# Chapter 27
## BREE

"Try not to get blood on my onions!" Jace yells from the stove.

The kitchen hums with energy. Rhett's at the stove, his broad shoulders hunched as he leans over a simmering pot, stirring with the kind of focus that comes natural to him. Jace, moving to the counter and coming shoulder-to-shoulder with Theo who has moved on from tomatoes to chopping herbs with surgical precision while Jace makes exaggerated faces at every slice he cuts. Gray leans against the fridge, arms crossed, his sharp green eyes flicking between the chaos and me.

And me? I stand at the sink, rinsing off a cutting board that has seen better days, feeling out of place in this well-oiled machine. But they've let me help, and that's something. A small victory in a house where it feels like everyone's holding their breath around me.

The scent of garlic and onions mingles with the faint aroma of bread warming in the oven. It's comforting, grounding, and so different from the empty hum of my old apartment, where dinner meant instant noodles or toast and the only sound was the faint buzz of the fridge. I glance at the others, watching the easy rhythm they've fallen into. This shouldn't feel like home. I shouldn't feel like I belong here.

Jace catches me watching and grins, his blue eyes crinkling at the corners. "You're up next, Bree. I hope you're ready to taste-test the masterpiece I've been slaving over."

Theo snorts without looking up from his chopping. "Slaving? You've barely done anything."

"Excuse me, chef extraordinaire, but I think someone forgot who's in charge of the main dish," Jace fires back, brandishing a wooden spoon like a sword. "I'm about to revolutionize your taste buds."

Rhett glances over his shoulder, a slow smile tugging at the corner of his mouth. "Pretty sure you said that last week. How'd that turn out again?"

"Okay, first of all, that lasagna was an experiment—"

"A disaster," Gray cuts in, his tone dry. "You set the smoke alarm off three times."

"I was testing its reliability," Jace says with mock indignation, winking at me when I finally crack a small smile.

The banter swirls around me, light and warm, like the steam rising from Rhett's pot. And yet, there's a weight under my ribs that won't lift. I grip the edge of the sink, my fingers pressing into the cool metal as their voices fade into the background.

They've done so much for me, and I'm grateful—more than they'll ever know. But I can't stay here forever. I can't keep letting them carry me. I need to figure out how to stand on my own, to save enough so I can finally find a place where my father's shadow doesn't stretch.

"Bree?" Gray's voice cuts through my thoughts, sharp but not unkind.

I blink, turning to find all four of them watching me. "What?"

"You okay?" Rhett asks, his brow furrowed with concern.

"Yeah." I force a smile, hoping it's convincing. "Just lost in thought."

"Don't go disappearing on us," Jace says lightly, though there's an edge to his tone. "Not when the fun part's about to start."

"What's the fun part?" I ask, though I already know. They've been hinting at this dinner for days now, building it up like some kind of sacred ritual.

Jace grins, holding up a plate like it's a prize. "The tasting, of course."

The door to the kitchen creaks open, and every head turns as Wes steps in. His dark curls are slightly damp, and his sharp, quiet gaze flicks over the room, taking in the chaos like he's weighing whether to dive in or let it pass.

"Sorry I'm late," he says simply, his voice low but warm enough to settle some of the tension in the room. His eyes land on me for a brief moment, and something flickers there—something that makes my breath catch before I can bury it.

"Perfect timing, broody," Jace says, clapping Wes on the back as he passes. "You missed my genius in action, but don't worry, I saved you a front-row seat for the masterpiece unveiling."

Wes doesn't answer, just moves to lean against the counter opposite me, his presence grounding in a way I can't explain. His dark eyes linger on me again, but this time, he doesn't say anything. He doesn't have to.

The kitchen hums back to life, Jace's exaggerated commentary mingling with Theo's quiet corrections and Rhett's steady presence at the stove. But Wes stays where he is, watching with that calm intensity that's always felt like a secret he's waiting to share.

And for a moment, as the smells of garlic and spices swirl around us, I let myself imagine that this could be normal. That I could be part of this, part of them. Even though I know better.

Because sooner or later, I'll have to leave. Sooner or later, this will have to end.

The dining table is chaos, but the kind of chaos that feels alive. Plates are passed back and forth, Jace narrating the "brilliance" of his contribution with exaggerated flair, while Rhett quietly refills everyone's glasses. Theo settles into his seat like he's orchestrating some grand feast, slicing the bread with careful precision. Gray sits at the head of the table, his eyes flicking between us, ever the quiet observer.

Wes slips into the chair next to me, his presence steady and grounding, though he hasn't said much since he walked in. He glances at my plate, then at me, like he's checking to see if I've eaten enough without actually asking.

I take a bite of whatever Jace slid onto my plate—something with chicken and a sauce that's probably fancier than he lets on—and savor the warmth spreading through me. It tastes like effort. Like care. Like a version of family I haven't let myself believe in for a long time.

"This," Jace says, pointing his fork at Rhett, "is why I should cook more often."

Rhett snorts, leaning back in his chair. "You assembled ingredients, Jace. The oven did most of the work."

"And yet, here you are, enjoying the fruits of my labor," Jace fires back, flashing a grin. "Theo, back me up."

Theo doesn't even look up from his plate. "Your contribution was adequate."

"High praise," Wes murmurs, his voice dry but soft enough that it draws a flicker of a smile from me.

The banter carries on, warm and easy, but my stomach tightens as I sit there, my fork toying with the food on my plate. I should just say it. Rip off the bandage and deal with the fallout. But the words feel heavy, harder to push out than I'd expected.

Gray catches my hesitation first. His sharp green eyes narrow slightly as he leans forward, elbows resting on the table. "What's on your mind, Bree?"

The table quiets, all their attention shifting to me in unison. It's a weight I'll never get used to—the intensity of their focus, the way they look at me like I'm something fragile and precious all at once.

"I'm going back to work tomorrow," I say, the words tumbling out faster than I mean them to.

The reaction is immediate.

"What?" Jace blurts, nearly dropping his fork.

"You're not ready," Rhett says, his voice firm but not unkind.

"Bree," Theo cuts in gently, setting his utensils down. "You've been through—"

"I know." My voice is sharper than I intended, and I take a deep breath, forcing myself to meet their eyes. "I know I've been through a lot. I know you're worried. But I need this."

"Do you?" Gray asks, his tone even but edged with challenge. "Or do you think you need it because you're afraid of leaning on us?"

"I can't lean on you forever," I say, the words burning in my throat. "I have to stand on my own."

"We're not asking you to lean on us forever," Wes says quietly, his voice cutting through the tension. "Just... for as long as you need to."

My chest tightens at the offer, at the steady way he looks at me, like he means it. Like he'd carry my weight forever if I let him.

"I appreciate everything you've done for me," I say, my voice softer now. "Really, I do. But this is something I have to do. For me."

The silence that follows feels heavy, but not hostile. Rhett runs a hand through his hair, exhaling sharply as if to steady himself. Jace looks down at his plate, his usual humor nowhere to be found. Theo's brow furrows, his lips pressing into a thin line.

Gray is the first to break the silence. "If you're going to work, you're not going alone."

"Gray—"

"Don't argue," he cuts me off, his tone brooking no room for debate. "You're not walking into that place by yourself. Not until we know everything's secure."

"I'll drive her," Jace says, finally looking up. "I have a showing near there tomorrow anyway."

Gray's eyes narrow slightly, but he nods. "Fine. But you call the second something feels off."

I glance between them, the weight of their protectiveness both comforting and suffocating. "It's just work. Nothing's going to happen."

"You don't know that," Rhett says, his voice quieter now but no less firm. "Not after everything we've found out."

The air feels thick again, the easy warmth of dinner replaced by something heavier. I push back from the table, my appetite gone, and stand. "I'll be fine," I say, trying to sound more confident than I feel. "Thank you for dinner. It was... amazing."

Without waiting for a response, I head toward the stairs, the weight of their worry pressing against my back. But in my chest, something else burns—a stubborn resolve.

*I have to do this. To save enough to find a place for myself, free from my father's shadow.*

But as I climb the stairs, the warmth of their voices follows me, making me wonder if I'm running from more than just the past.

# Chapter 28
## BREE

The truck smells faintly of leather and pine, a scent that's both comforting and suffocating. Jace taps his fingers on the steering wheel, humming along to a song playing softly through the speakers. The ride is quiet for the most part, just the low hum of the engine and the occasional crackle of the radio filling the space between us.

"You sure you're ready for this?" Jace asks, glancing over at me as we pull out of the driveway.

I nod, clutching my bag a little tighter in my lap. "I've been ready, Jace. It's just a shift. Nothing I haven't handled before."

His lips twitch, not quite a smile, but not full of doubt either. "Right. Just a shift. Nothing major at all. Definitely not your first time back after—"

"Don't," I cut him off, my voice sharper than I mean it to be. "Don't make it a thing."

"Fine, no 'thing.' Got it." He holds up one hand in mock surrender, though I catch the way his knuckles tighten around the wheel as he grabs it again.

The truck hums along the road, the trees blurring into a sea of green as we head toward Maple Grove. The mist lingers at the edges of the road, curling lazily around the tires like it's been following us the whole time.

"I'm just saying," Jace starts again after a beat, his tone softer this time, "you could've waited a few more days. Let yourself settle a bit more."

"I've had enough time," I reply, staring out the window at the passing fields. "Too much time."

My words hang between us, heavy and unspoken. Jace doesn't push, which is surprising for him. Instead, he changes the subject, his voice lightening as he nods toward the dashboard.

"So, the first family dinner didn't scare you off?"

I smirk despite myself. "I've survived worse."

"High praise," he says, grinning. "You know, if you play your cards right, I might just let you be the new reigning champion of 'best curry.'"

I roll my eyes, but the banter eases the knot in my chest. It's been like this with Jace since we were kids—his easy charm balancing out my sharp edges.

"Thanks for driving me," I say after a pause, my voice quieter.

He glances at me, his grin softening into something more genuine. "Always."

The mist thickens as we near the turn for Maple Grove, coiling along the ditches like it's waiting for something. I catch myself staring at it, the way it seems to almost glow in the early morning light, and quickly look away.

Jace pulls into the parking lot, the truck rumbling to a stop. He shifts into park, turning to face me fully. "You're sure you don't want me to wait? I've got a showing not far from here, but I can swing back if you need a ride."

"I'll be fine," I say, pulling on the strap of my bag. "You've already done enough."

"It's not about what I've done, Bree," he says, his voice dropping. "It's about making sure you're okay."

I swallow hard, the weight of his concern pressing against my chest. "I'll be fine," I repeat, forcing a smile. "Go sell your house."

He studies me for a moment longer before nodding. "Text me if you need anything, yeah?"

"Yeah."

I open the door, the cool morning air brushing against my skin as I step out. The mist seems to thicken as I walk toward the entrance, curling around my ankles like a persistent shadow. I don't look back, even though I can feel Jace's eyes on me until I disappear inside.

I have to do this. For myself. For Mrs. Henderson. And, if I'm being honest, to save enough to finally get out from under my father's shadow.

The familiarity of the nursing home hits me immediately—its too-bright fluorescents, the antiseptic tang in the air, the faint hum of conversation from the common room. I make it three steps past the receptionist's desk before I hear my name.

"Well, if it isn't Bree Holloway."

I turn, my bag on my shoulder slipping slightly as I come face-to-face with Jason, his smirk as irritatingly smug as I remember.

"Jason."

He grins, that same cocky tilt to his mouth that used to make my stomach flip when I was seventeen. Now, it just makes my skin crawl.

"That's right," he drawls, his gaze dragging over me like he's cataloging every detail. "Didn't think you'd show your face here, not after what people are saying."

My fingers tighten on the strap of my bag, my knuckles whitening as I fight the urge to shove past him. "I don't have time for this, Jason."

"Oh, come on." He shifts, blocking my path, his grin widening. "Don't be like that. You've got time for everyone else, don't you? Thought maybe you'd saved some for me."

"Move," I snap, keeping my voice low. The last thing I need is for this to turn into a spectacle.

He doesn't move. Instead, he steps closer, his eyes narrowing in a way that sends a cold shiver down my spine. "You know, I've been hearing some interesting things lately."

My stomach churns, but I keep my expression neutral. "I'm not interested."

"Oh, I think you are." He leans in slightly, lowering his voice. "Phil's been talking. Your dad, too. They've got some real stories about you, Bree."

The words hit like a slap, and I stagger back a step, the tray wobbling in my hands. "What are you talking about?"

Jason smirks, his confidence growing with every inch I give him. "Phil told me all about you. Said you like it rough. That you like a man who takes control. Said you're not happy unless someone's got you pinned to the wall, making you feel... wanted."

My grip on my bag falters, I almost drop it. The mist begins to stir at the edges of my vision, faint and restless, but Jason doesn't notice. He steps closer, his hand brushing against my arm, and I jerk back as if burned.

"Don't touch me," I snap, my voice sharper now.

His grin doesn't falter. If anything, it grows. "Relax, Bree. I'm just saying... if you're handing out pieces of yourself, don't forget the people who've been waiting the longest."

The mist surges, cold and sharp, curling around my ankles. Jason shivers slightly, finally noticing the sudden drop in temperature. He glances around, a flicker of unease crossing his face.

"What the hell?" he mutters, rubbing his arms.

I don't wait for him to recover. My legs carry me forward before my brain catches up, my shoulder knocking into his as I pass. My bag swings, but I don't stop until I'm in the staff lounge, the door slamming shut behind me.

I throw my bag on the counter, my uniform half falling out, but I barely notice. My hands are trembling, my breath coming too fast, too shallow. Jason's words echo in my head, pulling me back to Phil's leering face, my father's cruel whispers. The mist lingers near the door, curling protectively, but it does nothing to ease the nausea churning in my stomach.

They've poisoned everything. Every relationship, every memory. Jason was my first boyfriend. But I never gave him what he really wanted, no matter how much he pushed.. He was kind, sweet, even protective—until my father got to him. Until Phil twisted the narrative. Now he looks at me like I'm nothing more than an object to be used and discarded.

The words echo in my head, louder than they should: *You're a tease, Bree. Always have been.*

I press my palms flat against the counter, the cool metal biting into my skin as I try to steady myself. My chest tightens, every breath jagged. They'll never stop. Not until there's nothing left of me to ruin.

The mist stirs at the edges of my vision, curling closer, brushing against my fingertips like it's trying to pull me back from the edge. I swear it feels warmer, softer, as if it's saying: *You're still here. You're still whole.*

But the doubt creeps in, insidious and familiar. *Maybe they're right. Maybe that's all I'm worth. Maybe that's all I'm good for.*

My stomach churns as another thought surfaces, one I don't want to admit even to myself. *Is that why the guys want me there? Because they think I'm... that easy? That desperate?*

My breath catches, shame burning through me, hot and sharp. I grip the counter harder, forcing myself to face the thought. But even as it claws at me, another voice rises in defiance. *No.*

I shake my head, the motion sharp and instinctive. *They'd never.*

The certainty of it surprises me. Despite everything I've been through, everything I've been told, I can't picture Rhett, Wes, Theo, Jace, or Gray looking at me the way Jason did. They don't see me as something to use. They don't look through me. They look *at* me, like I'm something worth holding on to.

The mist swirls closer, encircling my wrists like a faint, protective embrace. I close my eyes, leaning into its quiet presence, letting it steady me. The coolness of the counter, the warmth of the mist, the steady rhythm of my breathing—all of it works to anchor me in the moment.

*They don't know everything.* The thought flickers, weak but insistent. *They don't know what's inside me. They don't get to break me again.*

When I open my eyes, the mist is still there, quiet and steady. I don't try to brush it away. I let it stay.

# Chapter 29
## BREE

The early morning light spills across the backyard, soft and golden, painting the dew-dappled grass in muted hues. My bare feet press into the cool earth as I sprint toward the blooms, my pulse pounding in my ears. The mist curls lazily at my ankles, a quiet companion as I skid to a stop near the oak tree.

They're glowing.

Not just blooming—glowing. Pale, iridescent light shimmers along the petals, shifting like sunlight on water. The sight steals my breath, holding me still. The delicate blossoms look like something from a dream, something not quite real.

I drop to my knees, fingers hovering over the nearest flower, tracing the edges of its strange, luminous petals. It's familiar, somehow, but different—like a memory blurred at the edges.

Then, it clicks. My breath stutters.

Daisies.

Not just any flowers. The ones I planted. The ones I wasn't sure would ever grow. The ones that, somehow, recognize me.

Warmth spreads through my fingertips as I brush against one of the blossoms, soft and pulsing, like the flowers breathe in rhythm with the mist. My breath catches, and for the first time in what feels like forever, I let myself feel... *joy*.

A quiet cough behind me shatters the moment, and I whirl around to see Rhett standing a few steps away, his hands tucked into his pockets. He looks like he just came back from a run—his dark t-shirt clings to his chest, and his hair sticks up at odd angles, still damp from sweat.

"Didn't mean to scare you," he says, his voice low and steady.

"You didn't," I manage, though my heart still races. I glance back at the glowing flowers, suddenly self-conscious. "I just... I wanted to check on them. I didn't know what the seeds actually were."

Rhett takes a few steps closer, his gaze dropping to the luminous blossoms. His brows furrow slightly, but there's no fear in his expression—just quiet curiosity.

"Guess they're not regular daisies, huh?"

I laugh softly, the sound catching me off guard. "No, definitely not."

He crouches beside me, his presence grounding me in a way I didn't expect. The morning breeze carries the faint scent of cedar and something warm and familiar—Rhett. "They're beautiful," he says after a moment, his voice softer now.

"Yeah," I whisper, looking at the flowers, then back at him.

The mist swirls around us, heavier now, curling around Rhett's legs like it's welcoming him. He doesn't flinch or pull away; he just watches me with that steady, unshakable gaze that makes my chest ache.

"I don't know why they're here," I admit, my voice barely audible. "But they feel... important. Like they're trying to tell me something."

Rhett's green eyes hold mine, and for a moment, the world narrows to just us. "Maybe they're trying to tell you you're important," he says quietly.

The words hit me harder than they should, stealing the air from my lungs. Before I can think, before I can second-guess myself, I lean forward and press my lips to his.

It's soft, tentative, over before I fully realize what I've done.

I pull back quickly, my heart hammering in my chest. "I—sorry. I don't know why I did that. I just—"

"Bree." His voice is quiet, steady, but there's something raw in it that makes me freeze.

I risk a glance up at him, my cheeks burning. His expression is unreadable, but his eyes... His eyes are anything but. They're soft and searching, like he's trying to understand something that doesn't make sense.

"You don't have to apologize," he says finally, his hand twitching at his side like he wants to reach for me but doesn't.

"I wasn't thinking," I mumble, my gaze dropping to the glowing daisies. "I just... I got caught up in the moment."

Rhett exhales slowly, and I feel the weight of his gaze like a physical thing. "Bree, you don't have to explain. I get it."

His words settle over me like a balm, easing the sharp edges of my embarrassment. I risk another glance at him, and this time, his lips curve into the faintest of smiles.

"Besides," he adds, his tone light but warm, "I've had worse ways to start my morning."

A surprised laugh escapes me, and the tension in my chest loosens just enough for me to breathe. The mist swirls thicker around us, wrapping the moment in quiet magic.

"Come on," Rhett says, rising to his feet and offering me a hand. "Let's get inside before Jace starts yelling about us missing breakfast."

I take his hand, his grip firm and steady as he pulls me to my feet. My heart's still racing, but it doesn't feel like fear. It feels… right.

As we head back to the house, I glance over my shoulder at the daisies. They're still glowing, their soft light blending with the mist.

*Maybe they are trying to tell me something.*

The warmth of the kitchen feels almost overwhelming after the coolness of the backyard. The smell of coffee and sizzling bacon wraps around me as I step inside, Rhett just a step behind me. Jace is at the stove, flipping pancakes with a flair that borders on theatrical. Gray sits at the table, scrolling through something on his phone, while Theo leans against the counter, sipping from a steaming mug.

"About time," Jace calls over his shoulder, his blue eyes narrowing playfully. "Thought you two got lost in the backyard."

"Bree was admiring her gardening skills," Rhett replies, his voice steady but carrying the barest hint of something I can't quite name.

I glance at him sharply, but his expression is calm, unreadable.

"The daisies?" Theo asks, his interest piqued.

I nod, sliding into a chair at the table. "They're… different."

Gray's gaze lifts from his phone, sharp and assessing. "Different how?"

"They're glowing," Rhett says, leaning against the fridge. He folds his arms, his green eyes flicking to me briefly before settling on Theo. "Like, actually glowing."

Theo sets his mug down, his brows drawing together in thought. "Glowing how? Bioluminescence or something else?"

I shrug, avoiding their curious gazes. "I don't know. They're just… not normal. But it's probably nothing."

"Nothing," Jace echoes, setting a plate of pancakes on the table. "Because glowing flowers are totally nothing. Happens all the time."

I force a smile, grateful when Rhett changes the subject by reaching for the coffee pot. But I can feel their attention lingering, like they're filing the daisies away as another thing to figure out. Another mystery tied to me.

"Sit," Jace commands, nudging Theo toward the table. "You too, Rhett. Breakfast is served, and I expect full reviews."

The early morning light catches on Gray's sharp green eyes as he watches me from across the table, his expression unreadable. The line of his jaw looks even harder in the soft glow filtering through the window, and for a second, I feel pinned by the weight of his gaze.

Jace sits to my left, his easy smile curling at the corner of his mouth as he nudges a plate of pancakes toward me. "Eat up, Bree. Can't have you wasting away on us." His bright blue eyes twinkle with mischief, but there's a flicker of something deeper beneath his usual charm.

Theo leans back in his chair, fingers wrapped around his mug of coffee. His dark hair falls across his forehead as he tilts his head, studying me in that quiet, analytical way of his. It's like he's trying to piece me together, one careful observation at a time.

Rhett, seated beside me, shifts slightly, his broad shoulders brushing mine. The tee shirt he's wearing reveals the strong lines of his forearms, the tan of his skin against the black fabric a sharp contrast. His green eyes flick to me, steady and grounding, before dropping back to his plate.

"How was work yesterday?" Gray asks, breaking me away from my thoughts.

My fork freezes halfway to my mouth. "It was fine," I say quickly, too quickly.

Gray's sharp gaze narrows slightly, but he doesn't push. Not yet.

"Fine?" Jace prompts, raising an eyebrow. "That's it? Come on, Bree, give us something to work with here."

"It's work," I say, forcing a lightness into my voice. "Same as always."

But it's not. Jason's voice still echoes in my head, his words cutting deeper than I want to admit.

*"You're just like Phil said."*

*"Not happy unless someone's got you pinned to the wall."*

The words coil around my throat like barbed wire. I swallow hard, but they don't go away.

I stare at my plate, suddenly nauseous. The food that had smelled so comforting earlier now feels like lead in my stomach.

"You're lying," Theo says softly, his tone careful but unyielding.

My head snaps up, and my heart stutters at the weight of their combined attention.

"I'm not lying," I protest, but the words sound hollow, even to me.

"You're hiding something," Rhett says, his voice low and steady, like he's testing the waters.

My pulse quickens, and I grip the edge of the table to keep my hands from shaking. "It's nothing. Just... a long day. That's all."

They don't look convinced. Jace exchanges a glance with Theo, who shifts in his seat like he's weighing his next words. Gray leans back, his arms crossing over his chest as he studies me with an intensity that makes me want to squirm.

Rhett's voice cuts through the silence. "Bree, you don't have to tell us everything. But don't expect us to believe 'nothing.'"

The words hang in the air, heavy and pointed. My throat tightens, and I look down at my plate, avoiding their gazes.

"It's not a big deal," I say finally, my voice barely above a whisper. "Just someone I used to know. An old... friend."

"Friend," Jace repeats, his tone laced with skepticism. "And this 'friend' made your day 'fine.'"

"Jace," Theo warns, his tone a soft reprimand, though his sharp gaze doesn't leave me.

But I can feel their worry, their frustration, pressing in around me. They want answers, want to help, and it's tearing me apart that I can't let them. That I can't let myself.

Jason's voice echoes in my mind, sharp and condescending: *You're just like Phil said. You're not happy unless someone's got you pinned to the wall.*

My stomach churns, and I grip the edge of the table tighter, focusing on the wood grain beneath my fingertips. *They don't know that. They don't know everything.*

"It's not worth talking about," I say, forcing my voice to steady. "Can we just... not do this right now?"

The silence that follows feels suffocating. Rhett exchanges a glance with Theo, who looks like he wants to press further but stays quiet. Jace leans back in his chair, his lips twitching like he's biting back a dozen questions. And Gray just watches, his arms crossed and his sharp green eyes cutting through me like he's trying to dismantle every wall I'm clinging to.

"It's not nothing," Rhett says finally, his voice low. There's no anger, just a quiet conviction that makes my throat tighten. "But okay. For now."

The weight in his words is palpable. *For now.* A temporary truce. A promise that this conversation isn't over.

Jace exhales sharply, breaking the tension. "You're lucky I make amazing pancakes," he mutters, but the humor feels forced, his blue eyes still shadowed as he looks at me.

I pick up my fork, though the thought of eating makes my stomach twist. Across the table, Theo shifts in his chair, watching me with the kind of quiet intensity that's impossible to ignore. The analytical part of my brain knows he's cataloging every detail—my posture, my tone, the way my hands tremble when I think no one's looking.

But someone's always looking. Always watching. That thought flickers darkly in the back of my mind, and I shove it down, forcing myself to swallow a bite of pancake.

I glance toward the hallway, where the faint sound of movement upstairs draws my attention. "Where's Wes?" I ask, grateful for the distraction.

"Sleeping in," Jace answers with a shrug, though his gaze doesn't leave me. "Late night at the bar."

"Classic Wes," he adds, grinning faintly. "Broody, mysterious, and running on four hours of sleep like it's a lifestyle choice."

"Better than you running on caffeine and bad decisions," Theo mutters into his coffee, though the corners of his mouth twitch.

The banter washes over me, light and familiar, but I feel the absence of Wes like a missing piece of the puzzle. He's always been the quiet one, the steady one, but even now, I wonder if he's staying away because he can sense how close I am to breaking.

The mist curls faintly at the edges of the window, and I glance at it for a moment too long. Rhett follows my gaze, his brows furrowing slightly, but he doesn't say anything. None of them do.

"It's not forever," I murmur under my breath, not realizing I've spoken aloud until Rhett's green eyes flick back to me, sharp with curiosity.

"What's not forever?" he asks, his voice quiet but steady.

I shake my head quickly, forcing a smile. "Nothing. Just... nothing."

They don't press, but the tension lingers like an unspoken promise. Jason's words, Phil's threats, my father's shadow—they're all still there, heavy and suffocating. But for now, I keep them to myself, swallowing the bitterness like a stone lodged in my throat.

# Chapter 30
## GRAY

The attic feels different tonight, heavier somehow. Maybe it's the weight of everything unsaid, or maybe it's just me. The others file in one by one, their footsteps muted against the floorboards. I shut the door behind us, leaning against it for a moment longer than necessary.

Rhett stands by the window, his broad shoulders outlined against the faint glow of the moonlight. Jace collapses onto the old loveseat, his usual energy subdued but still there in the restless tapping of his fingers against his knee. Theo claims the armchair by the corner, his sharp gaze already scanning the room like he's solving a puzzle no one else can see. Wes lingers by the far wall, quiet as always, his arms crossed over his chest like he's holding himself together.

It's not lost on me that we've fallen into these roles again—the careful dance of who stands where, who speaks first, who waits.

"She kissed me," Rhett says suddenly, breaking the silence.

Four heads snap toward him, mine included.

Jace straightens on the loveseat, his easy demeanor replaced with something sharper. "Wait—what?"

Theo leans forward in his chair, his brow furrowing. "When?"

"This morning. By the daisies." Rhett turns to face us, his green eyes steady but conflicted. "She... she pulled back right after. Apologized. Said she wasn't thinking."

"What did you say?" I ask, my voice coming out rougher than I intend.

Rhett's hand curls into a fist against the windowsill, but his voice stays steady. "I told her she didn't have to explain. That I got it." His gaze drops, his shoulders tense like he's bracing for judgment. "She was caught up in the moment, that's all."

Jace lets out a low whistle, running a hand through his hair. "Caught up in the moment? That's what you're going with?"

"She kissed me," Rhett snaps, his green eyes blazing. "And then she apologized. What was I supposed to do—push her for more? She doesn't need that. She doesn't need me making it harder for her."

"She doesn't need space, Rhett," Theo says evenly, though his tone carries a hint of frustration. "She needs to know she's allowed to feel something good without apologizing for it."

"She needs to know she's not alone," Wes adds, his voice quiet but resolute. "And right now, she doesn't."

"No, she doesn't," Theo says evenly, though his tone carries more weight than usual. "But she also doesn't need mixed signals. If she kissed you, it means she's trying to trust us."

"She's already trusting us," Wes cuts in, his voice quieter but no less intense. "She let me sit with her the other morning. Let me talk to her about... about things I never thought I'd say out loud." He pauses, his jaw tightening. "But she doesn't think she deserves us. Any of us."

The room falls silent again, the truth of Wes's words hitting harder than anyone wants to admit.

"Like when I told her the attic was hers," Wes continues, his tone measured but raw. "She said she didn't deserve it."

Theo leans forward slightly, his hands clasped. "We've all seen it, haven't we? The way she looks at us. Like we're these impossible things she can't let herself have. Like we're—" He exhales sharply, the words hanging unfinished.

"Too much for her," Jace finishes, his voice softer now. "But not because she doesn't want us. Because she doesn't think she's enough."

·"She doesn't think she's enough because of them," Rhett growls, his knuckles whitening against the windowsill. "Phil. Her father. They've poisoned everything. Every thought she has about herself."

"And we're here, trying to fix it," Wes murmurs, his voice carrying that quiet steel that makes you listen even when he's barely speaking.

"We all love her." Wes says it like a truth he's known forever but has never dared to say aloud.

The words settle over the room like a punch to the gut. No one moves, no one speaks.

"It's always been her," I say finally, the truth scraping out of me like glass. "Since we were kids. It's always been her."

Theo nods, his dark eyes steady but full of something I can't quite name. "Yeah. It has."

Jace leans back against the loveseat, his head tipped back like he's trying to find the right words on the ceiling. "You don't think... you don't think she'd ever need all of us, do you?"

The question hangs heavy in the air. It's not something we've ever said aloud, not something we've ever let ourselves think too much about.

"Would that even work?" Rhett asks, his voice low. "All of us? Together?"

"Why not?" Jace says, his voice tinged with something almost hopeful. "We've shared everything else. We've built a life together, built this house, built..." He trails off, gesturing vaguely toward the attic around us. "Why not this?"

"She'd have to choose," Rhett mutters, though there's no conviction in his tone. "Wouldn't she?"

Wes shakes his head slowly, his dark eyes unreadable. "Maybe she doesn't have to."

The mist swirls around our feet, heavier now, curling in the dim light. I glance toward the door, half expecting it to react like Wes said it did when Bree touched it. But nothing happens.

"She doesn't even know how much she means to us," My voice raw with emotions I can't seem to push down. "She thinks we see her the way they did. Like she's..." I pause, clenching my jaw because I don't want to say the words, but I have to. "Like she's a thing to be used and discarded." The mist stirs, a faint ripple across the floorboards, then stills again.

"She'll figure it out," Theo says quietly, though there's something in his tone that makes me look at him sharply. "She has to."

But the words feel hollow, even as he says them. Because we all know Bree doesn't believe in her own worth. Not yet.

"Let's not screw this up," I say finally, my voice rough but steady. "Not for her. Not for us."

The others nod, the unspoken promise settling between us like a fragile thread.

But as the mist curls thicker, I can't shake the feeling that we're already on borrowed time. And I wonder—when the moment comes, when Bree finally hears what she's not ready to hear—will we lose her for good?

# Chapter 31
## BREE

The house feels too big at night. Too quiet. Even the soft creaks of the old floors sound louder, stretching the silence into something oppressive.

I sit up in bed, the blanket pooling around my waist. Sleep has been elusive all week, each restless night tangling my thoughts until they're impossible to sort through. Tonight is no different. The weight in my chest refuses to ease, even as I stare at the faint glow of the moonlight spilling through the window.

*The attic.*

The thought drifts through my mind unbidden, pulling at me. I can't explain it, but I've been drawn to that space ever since I first stepped inside. Like it's calling me back, like it's trying to tell me something I'm not ready to hear.

Sliding out of bed, I tug Rhett's hoodie tighter around me, the hem brushing against my thighs. My feet move almost on their own, the cool wood floor creaking softly under my steps as I make my way toward the attic stairs.

The mist stirs at my feet, curling and coiling like it knows where I'm going. I don't question it. Not tonight.

As I near the attic door, the faint sound of voices filters through the quiet, muffled but unmistakable. I freeze, my heart kicking up a notch.

The guys must be up there. Talking about something serious, judging by the low, tense tones.

I should turn around. Go back to my room and pretend I never heard anything. But something keeps me rooted to the spot, my breath shallow as I lean closer. Just a little. Just enough to catch a few words.

"We see her the way they did. Like she's..." Gray's voice cuts through the stillness, low and heavy with frustration. He stops, his jaw clenching audibly in the pause. "Like she's a thing to be used and discarded."

My chest tightens, a cold chill creeping up my spine. My heart pounds as the words echo in my head, louder than the faint hum of their conversation.

A thing to be used. Discarded.

Jason's voice sneers through my memory, sharp and cruel: *You're just like Phil said. You're not happy unless someone's got you pinned to the wall.*

"She'll figure it out," Theo's voice follows, quieter but no less damning.

The air feels heavier, pressing down on me as I back away from the door, each step slow and careful. My pulse roars in my ears, drowning out the rest of their conversation.

*They think the same.*

My hands tremble, gripping the fabric of Rhett's hoodie as if it can somehow shield me from the sharp sting of their words. The mist stirs around my feet, colder now, as if sensing my distress. I don't know if it's trying to comfort me or keep me from running, but I can't stay here.

I have to leave.

Before they throw me away, before they say the things I can't bear to hear out loud. Not from them. I have to leave, now.

Back in my room, I press my back against the door, sliding down until I'm sitting on the floor. My thoughts spiral, Jason's accusations twisting together with Gray's words until I can't tell them apart. *A thing to be used. Discarded.* That's all I've ever been. That's all they see.

The mist coils tighter around me, its touch colder now, more insistent. My breath hitches as I press my palms to my face, trying to stop the tears that threaten to spill.

I knew I didn't belong here—I didn't expect them to prove it. I just wish I hadn't let myself hope.

Now I know better.

The thought solidifies, sharp and resolute, cutting through the haze of my panic. I wipe at my cheeks and take a shaky breath, the beginnings of a plan forming in the back of my mind.

I won't let anyone do this to me. Not again.

The room feels smaller now, the walls pressing in like they know what I'm about to do. The moonlight slices through the curtains, too bright, too exposing. My chest tightens as I grab the box from the corner of the room—the one filled with the remnants of my life.

I set it on the bed, my hands shaking as I open it. The sight of its contents—pressed daisies, movie stubs, scrawled notes from years long gone—makes my stomach churn. These were pieces of something I thought I'd never lose. But now, all I see are reminders of how stupid I've been. How naïve.

My hand hovers over the pressed flowers, the edges brittle and delicate. Jason's voice echoes in my head again. Phil's sneer. My father's contempt. The sharp weight of Gray's words presses harder against my ribs: She's a thing to be used and discarded.

With a sharp inhale, I grab the daisy, the movie stubs, the notes, and rip them into pieces. The sound of tearing paper fills the silence of the room, each shred a catharsis that burns as much as it soothes. When I'm done, the bed is covered in fragments of memories, scattered like ashes.

But I don't cry.

My gaze shifts to the other side of the room, where the pretty, soft things the guys bought for me are neatly arranged. It's too much. I don't have nice things. That's not in the cards for me. It makes my chest ache, my stomach twist, because I let myself believe it, even for a moment.

Not anymore.

All I see is proof that I was stupid enough to think this was real. That they cared because I mattered, not because I'm some broken thing to be pitied. To be fixed.

My gaze drags over the stack of books Theo brought me, the silky pajamas Jace insisted on, the throw blanket Rhett draped over the chair with quiet care. And suddenly, all of it feels wrong. Heavy. Suffocating.

This is what I'm worth? The thought claws its way up before I can stop it. Maybe I should be surprised they thought it would cost this much for me to spread my legs.

The bile rises in my throat, sharp and sour, as Jason's voice cuts through my mind like a whip: You're not happy unless someone's got you pinned to the wall.

My fingers curl into fists, my nails digging into my palms as I force myself to look away from the things they gave me. It all feels poisoned now, warped by the words I overheard, by the shadow of my father's voice and Phil's threats. By Jason's cruelty.

They're all the same. Aren't they? Trying to buy pieces of me, pretending it's care when all they really want is to own what's left.

My chest heaves, my breath shaky as I shove the thought away. It doesn't matter. None of it matters.

My hands tremble as I move to the small drawer where my journal sits. This, at least, is mine. It's the only thing that holds the truth of what I've endured, unfiltered and untouched by anyone else. I clutch it to my chest before slipping it into the small bag I'd brought with me. My hands work quickly, methodically: my single spare outfit, my work scrubs, the essentials. That's it.

I glance toward the window, the faint glow of the daisies still visible in the distance. They shimmer like they're trying to tell me something, but I can't let myself listen. Not now. Maybe not ever.

The mist curls at the edges of the door as I reach for the handle, coiling tighter as if it's trying to stop me. Its chill bites against my ankles, a silent protest I don't have the strength to acknowledge.

"I have to go," I whisper, the words breaking in the still air. "I can't... stay."

The mist curls around my ankle, tighter now, like it's trying to hold me back. I hesitate, just for a second. But then it loosens, retreating like it knows I've already made my choice.

With one last glance at the room, at the torn remnants of my past scattered across the bed, and the thoughtful things I now see as chains, I swallow the lump in my throat and leave.

The door clicks shut behind me. Discarded. I guess I should be happy they didn't use me first.

# Chapter 32
## WES

The sun filters through the kitchen windows, casting long shadows across the counter. The smell of coffee fills the air, but it does little to cut through the tension simmering beneath the surface. Jace sits at the island, absently drumming his fingers on the countertop, his usual energy subdued. Rhett leans against the sink, his arms crossed, staring out the window like it might hold answers.

"Quiet morning," Jace remarks, his tone too light to be genuine. He glances at the clock. "Bree's sleeping late today."

"She mentioned an earlier shift, didn't she?" Theo's voice is calm, but there's an edge to it, subtle but unmistakable.

I glance up from my seat at the table, the unease I've been trying to push aside curling tighter in my chest. Bree's never been one to oversleep. If anything, she's always up before the rest of us, moving through the morning like a ghost trying not to be seen.

"I'll check on her," Rhett offers, already moving toward the stairs.

The silence in the kitchen thickens as we wait. My fingers tighten around my mug, the ceramic cool against my skin. Something feels wrong.

Rhett steps into the kitchen. Stops short. His jaw tightens, his movements stiff. The silence stretches—too long, too heavy.

"She's gone."

Jace freezes mid-drum, his hand falling still. "Gone?"

"Her room's empty." Rhett's gaze flickers to each of us, searching for answers we don't have. "She took her bag. Only the things she came with are missing."

Theo is already on his feet, moving toward the stairs with purpose. "What about her other things?"

"Scattered," Rhett mutters, running a hand through his hair. "Torn, shredded—like she didn't want to leave anything behind for us to find."

Something cold settles in my stomach, a weight that presses against my ribs as we follow Rhett upstairs. Bree's room feels hollow, the air heavy with the absence of her presence. The bed is made, but the chaos she left behind—shreds of paper, fragments of memories—is impossible to ignore.

Theo crouches by the bed, his hand brushing over a torn piece of a daisy, now brittle and lifeless. Jace stands by the door, his jaw tight, eyes scanning the room like he's piecing together a puzzle he doesn't want to solve.

"She didn't just leave," I say, my voice breaking the silence. "She ran."

The words hang in the air, heavy and undeniable. My gaze catches on the dresser where Jace's carefully chosen clothes still sit, untouched. The reading lamp he picked out, the books Theo brought her - everything we tried to give her, left behind like evidence of something she couldn't bear to keep.

"Last night," Gray says suddenly from the doorway, his sharp eyes taking in the scene. His jaw tightens. "The attic."

A beat of silence. The realization crashes in like a cold slap of water.

"She must have heard us."

*Fuck.*

"Would explain this." Theo gestures to the torn remnants on her bed, his voice tight. "Question is, what exactly did she hear?"

The silence that follows feels suffocating. I think of everything we discussed up there - about feelings none of us have voiced to her, about choices and lack of choices, about how much we all...

"Doesn't matter what she heard," Rhett cuts in, his jaw clenched. "She ran. Again. Like she always does when things get..."

"Real?" Gray finishes, but there's no judgment in his tone. Just a bone-deep understanding that makes my chest ache.

I move to the window, drawn by something I can't explain. The daisies still glow faintly in the morning light, untouched by whatever drove her to destroy everything else. The mist curls around them, restless and cold, like it's trying to tell us something we're too slow to understand.

"We need to find her," Jace says, but uncertainty threads through his voice. "Before she..."

"Convinces herself she was right to run?" I finish quietly. "That whatever she thinks she heard was proof she doesn't belong here?"

No one answers. Because what can we say? That we've been dancing around this thing between all of us for years? That maybe the idea of choosing - or not having to choose - was too much for her to face?

"She'll have gone somewhere she feels safe," Theo says finally, his analytical mind already working through possibilities. "Somewhere she can process whatever she thinks she discovered."

Or somewhere she can hide, I think but don't say. Somewhere she can build her walls back up, convince herself that running was the only choice she had.

The morning sun catches on the torn pieces of her past, and I wonder if this is how it always ends with Bree - not with a fight or a goodbye, but with scattered fragments of memories she couldn't bear to keep.

# Chapter 33
## BREE

The city feels different at dawn. Empty streets stretch out before me, street lights flickering as the sky shifts from black to navy to a pale, sickly gray. My feet carry me forward without direction, each step taking me further from the warmth I let myself believe in.

The mist follows, curling around my ankles like it's trying to slow me down. I ignore it, just like I ignore the ache in my chest that threatens to crack me open.

*A thing to be used and discarded.*

Gray's words echo in my head, twisting together with every other voice that's ever told me what I'm worth. Jason sneering about what Phil said. My father's cruel whispers. The weight of their judgment presses against my ribs until I can barely breathe.

I clutch my bag closer, the familiar worn strap grounding me as I turn down another empty street. My scrubs shift inside, reminding me that I still have work later. Still have to pretend everything's normal, that I'm not running from the only place that ever felt like...

No. I can't think about that.

The pale morning light catches on something ahead - the iron gates of Oakwood Cemetery. My feet slow, recognition settling in my bones. The last time I was here, I was the only one at her funeral. The priest mumbled something about finding peace, but the wind stole the words before I could hear them. I just stood there, watching the dirt cover another life no one cared to remember.

*Just like me.*

The gates are still locked, but there's a gap in the fence that neighborhood kids use to sneak in. I slip through without thinking, the rust rough against my palm. The mist follows, thicker now, almost protective as I wind my way through the weathered headstones.

Mrs. Henderson's grave is easy to find - still fresh, the dirt darker than the surrounding ground. I sink down beside it, my legs folding under me like they can't hold my weight anymore.

"I messed up," I whisper to the silent stone. "I let myself believe... I thought maybe..."

But I can't finish. The words stick in my throat, sharp and jagged. Because how do I explain that I let myself hope? That for a moment, I actually believed I could have something real, something good?

*"They've got some real stories about you, Bree,"* Jason's voice sneers in my memory. *"Phil told me all about you."*

My fingers dig into the damp earth beside the grave, anchoring me as the first rays of sun spill across the cemetery. The mist curls closer, and for a second I swear it feels warmer, like it's trying to comfort me.

"You would have told me I was being stupid," I say to Mrs. Henderson's headstone, a bitter laugh catching in my throat. "Running away instead of facing them. But you didn't hear what I heard. You didn't see..."

See what? The careful way they watched me? The gifts they gave me, each one chosen to make me feel safe, wanted? The space they built just for me?

*No.* I squeeze my eyes shut, forcing back the tears that threaten to fall. Those weren't gifts. They were chains, pretty things meant to keep me docile until they decided what they wanted from me.

The sun climbs higher, warming the cool stone beneath my palm. I should move, find somewhere else to hide until my shift starts. But something keeps me here, rooted to this quiet corner of the cemetery where the only judgment comes from silent granite angels.

A bird calls somewhere nearby, the sound sharp in the morning stillness. The mist shifts restlessly, and I catch a faint glow in my peripheral vision. For a moment, I think it's the daisies I left behind, but when I turn, there's nothing there.

Just shadows and stone and the weight of everything I'm trying to outrun.

I pull my journal from my bag, running my fingers over the worn leather cover. So many secrets hidden in these pages, so many truths I've never been able to say out loud. The guys never asked to read it, never pushed to know what I wrote about in the quiet hours when sleep wouldn't come.

Maybe that should have told me something.

But it doesn't matter now. None of it does. Because in the end, everyone wants something from me. Everyone has a price they think I'm worth.

And I'm done letting people decide my value.

The morning light catches on my mother's ring, still on my finger after all these years. Another woman who ran when staying got too hard. Maybe that's my inheritance - the need to disappear before anyone can see how broken I really am.

A siren wails in the distance, reminding me that the world is waking up. Soon the cemetery will fill with groundskeepers and mourners, and I'll have to find somewhere else to hide.

But for now, I let myself stay. Let the mist wrap around me like a shield against the growing light. Let myself pretend, just for a moment, that I'm not my mother's daughter, running from the only people who might have actually...

No. I can't finish that thought.

Because some things aren't meant for people like me.

Some stories only end one way. I just wish mine had been different.

# Chapter 34
## RHETT

I slam the truck door harder than I mean to, the sound echoing through the empty street. My hands grip the steering wheel like it's the only thing keeping me together, knuckles white, nails digging into my palms.

Where the hell is she?

I've been driving for hours—through the city, the neighborhoods I know she'd never go, the places I hoped to God she wouldn't. Every corner feels like a dead end, every familiar landmark a reminder that I've failed her. Again.

I should've seen this coming. Should've known she'd run. It's what she does when things get too real, when the weight of everything she carries gets too much to bear. But knowing doesn't make it any easier.

Doesn't make it hurt any less.

"Damn it!" My fist slams against the steering wheel, the sharp pain a welcome distraction from the hollow ache in my chest. I can feel the frustration bubbling over, hot and blinding, but there's nowhere to put it. Nowhere to direct it except at myself.

I pull into a random parking lot and park haphazardly, my hands trembling as I grip the wheel. My breath comes in short, sharp bursts, and I press my forehead against the cool leather, trying to pull myself together.

But the image of her room—hollow, emptied out—burns in my mind like a brand.

She didn't just leave. She took only what she came with. Every single thing we gave her—the books, the clothes, the little comforts we thought might make her feel safe—she left behind. Like they never meant anything.

The thought twists something sharp and painful in my gut. Because maybe she didn't just leave to protect herself. Maybe she left to prove she never belonged.

Maybe she left because she didn't trust us. Because she thought we were just like—

I slam the door open and step out, pacing the lot like a caged animal. The air is cool against my overheated skin, but it doesn't do a damn thing to settle the storm inside me. I run a hand through my hair, yanking at the ends like the pain might drag me out of this spiral.

Where the hell could she have gone?

I've checked the hospital, her old apartment, every goddamn coffee shop within a ten-mile radius. No sign of her. No one's seen her. It's like she's disappeared, like the earth opened up and swallowed her whole.

I shove my hands into my pockets, my fingers brushing against the keys I've carried for years. The ones that open every door to this damn house. The one she didn't slam shut behind her.

The house.

Before I know it, I'm back in the driveway, the truck barely in park before I'm out, striding toward the backyard like the answers are waiting for me there. Because that's where she was happiest. That's where she felt most like... her.

The daisies catch my eye immediately, their faint glow like a beacon in the growing dusk. My breath catches, and for a moment, the fury in my chest softens into something more painful. Something more desperate.

I drop to my knees in the damp grass, the cool earth grounding me as I stare at the flowers she planted. They're still glowing, but it's different now—fainter, like they're losing their light. Like they're missing her too.

"What do you want me to do?" My voice breaks in the stillness, raw and unsteady. "Where is she? How do I—" I stop, swallowing hard against the lump in my throat. "How do I bring her back?"

The mist stirs around me, curling tighter, colder, almost restless. I reach out without thinking, my fingers brushing against one of the daisies. The warmth I felt before is barely there now, a ghost of what it was.

I pluck it carefully, the stem trembling in my hand. The glow fades almost entirely, and for a second, it feels like I've lost her all over again. Like this is the last piece of her, slipping through my fingers.

"Bree," I whisper, the word catching in my throat.

I stand slowly, the daisy cradled in my palm, its light faint but persistent. My chest tightens as I turn back toward the house, the weight of failure pressing heavy on my shoulders. But as I step forward, the light shifts—brighter now, spreading from the petals down the stem, wrapping around my fingers like a pulse.

The mist moves with it, swirling around my feet in a way that feels deliberate. Intentional.

My heart pounds as I take another step, and the light flares again, stronger this time. Guiding.

"Is this you?" My voice is barely audible, my fingers tightening around the daisy. "Are you—"

The light pulses again, pulling me toward the edge of the yard. The mist flows ahead of me, weaving through the grass like it knows where to go. Like it's leading me.

I don't hesitate. I don't question. I just follow.

Because if this is her, if this is the only way I can find her, I'm not stopping until I do.

The light grows brighter with every step, the daisy in my hand glowing like a tiny beacon. The mist swirls ahead of me, weaving between the trees as I follow its lead. My pulse pounds in my ears, each step quicker than the last.

I don't question where it's taking me anymore. The streets, the turns—they blur together, fading into the background. All that matters is the pull in my chest, the overwhelming sense that she's close.

The glow intensifies as the mist guides me toward a familiar iron gate—Oakwood Cemetery. My breath catches, my chest tightening as I push the gate open, the creak of iron breaking the stillness of the dawn.

I step inside, scanning the quiet rows of headstones. The morning sun casts long shadows across the uneven ground, the mist curling low around the stones. It feels heavier here, charged with something I can't name.

And then I see her.

A figure kneeling near a fresh grave, dark hair catching the faint light. My heart lurches, and I start toward her, the daisy glowing brighter in my hand as if urging me forward.

"Bree," I whisper, the name slipping from my lips like a prayer.

She doesn't move. The mist swirls thickly around her, obscuring the details, but I can see her shape, her stillness, the way her shoulders hunch against the chill. Relief floods through me, sharp and overwhelming, as I close the distance between us.

"Bree," I call again, louder this time.

The figure shifts, slowly turning toward me.

# Chapter 35
## BREE

The voice sends ice down my spine, sharp and unmistakable. My breath locks in my chest.

*No. No, no, no. Not here. Not now.*

But I know that voice. I know it in the same way I know nightmares.

Slowly, like my body is moving through water, I turn.

"Phil," I manage, my voice barely audible over the roar of my pulse.

He smirks, stepping closer, his hands stuffed casually into the pockets of his jacket like he has all the time in the world. "Nice to see you again, sweetheart. Thought we might have a little... chat."

My mouth goes dry as I take a step back, the fresh dirt of Mrs. Henderson's grave shifting beneath my feet. The mist surges around me, thicker now, like it's trying to form a barrier.

"What do you want?" I ask, trying to keep my voice steady.

"What do you think?" His tone is smooth, but the underlying menace sends a shiver through me. "You've been making quite the impression, Bree. Got a lot of people worried about what you might do next."

I swallow hard, my fists clenching at my sides. "I don't know what you're talking about."

He chuckles, the sound low and cold. "Oh, I think you do. See, your daddy's not too happy with you right now. Says you've been getting ideas above your station. And we can't have that, can we?"

My stomach churns, his words slicing through me like shards of glass. "Stay away from me."

"Now, now." Phil's grin widens, and he takes another step forward. The mist ripples between us, its glow intensifying like it's trying to hold him back. "No need to get feisty. I'm here to help, sweetheart. Just like your old man asked me to."

"Help?" The word tastes bitter on my tongue. "You mean like you helped last time? Is that what you call it?"

His smirk falters for a fraction of a second, but it's enough to fan the flames of my anger. My hands shake, and I take another step back, the cool stone of Mrs. Henderson's headstone pressing against my leg.

"You don't scare me," I lie, my voice trembling despite my best efforts.

Phil's eyes darken, and he leans forward slightly, his smirk replaced by something colder. "You should be scared, Bree. Because this time? There's no one here to save you."

The mist surges again, a sharp wind whipping through the cemetery. For a split second, I swear I see something in the haze—a shape, a shadow, something that doesn't belong.

But then Phil steps closer, and the moment shatters.

"You're not going anywhere, sweetheart," he says, his voice low and dangerous. "Not until we've had our little talk."

My heart pounds in my chest, every instinct screaming at me to move, to run, to fight. But I'm frozen, caught between the suffocating weight of his presence and the strange energy thrumming through the mist around me.

I glance toward the gates, my thoughts racing. If I can just get to the street, to somewhere public—

"Don't even think about it," Phil snaps, his tone sharp. "You think you can outrun me?"

I take a shaky breath, my gaze flickering back to him. "I think you're underestimating me."

The smirk returns, but there's something meaner behind it now. "Let's see about that."

The mist shifts, curling tighter around my legs as if trying to hold me in place. Or protect me. I don't know anymore. All I know is that I can't stay here.

"Last chance, Bree," Phil says, his voice soft but laced with menace. "Come quietly, or this gets messy."

I meet his gaze, my fear warring with the anger simmering just beneath the surface. My father sent him. My father, who has spent my entire life proving how little I'm worth.

The mist pulses again, brighter now, and I feel something shift deep inside me.

"Come and get me," I say, the words falling from my lips before I can think better of them.

Phil's smirk twists into something darker as he steps forward.

And I run.

The mist surges with me, curling and twisting like it's alive, like it's trying to shield me from the shadow chasing me through the graves. The ground blurs beneath my feet, the sound of Phil's footsteps pounding in my ears. The mist surges around me, curling and twisting like it's trying to shield me from the shadow at my back.

And then I hear it - another voice cutting through the morning air, sharp and familiar in a completely different way.

"BREE!"

My heart stutters. Rhett.

I stumble, caught between Phil behind me and the last person I want to see right now ahead of me. The mist swirls frantically, and for a moment I swear it glows brighter, like it's trying to tell me something.

But all I can think is: I can't let Phil hurt him.

I have to run. I have to get him away from Rhett. I have to—

The mist flares, curling tighter, almost like it's trying to tell me something.

But it's too late. I'm already moving.

# Chapter 36
## RHETT

"Bree—" The name dies in my throat as I catch sight of Phil steps from her, his face twisted with something dark and hungry. The daisy in my hand pulses brighter, almost hot against my palm, as fury floods through me.

Without taking my eyes off Phil, I slip my phone from my pocket, thumbing the screen until I feel it vibrate - Gray's contact. One ring, then silence. He'll understand.

"Well, isn't this touching," Phil sneers, his gaze flicking between us. "The hero arrives just in time."

I move forward slowly, deliberately placing myself between him and Bree. The mist coils around my feet, thicker than I've ever seen it, almost solid in its intensity.

"Rhett, don't—" Bree's voice cracks behind me. "Just go. Please."

"Not happening." My voice comes out low, deadly calm despite the rage burning in my chest. The kind of calm that comes before a storm.

Phil's smirk widens as he takes a step closer. "You hear that, sweetheart? Always trying to play the protector. But we both know what you really want from her, don't we?"

"Back off." I shift my stance, years of firefighter training kicking in as I assess the threat. He's bigger than me, but slower. Drunk, probably. Dangerous.

"Or what?" Phil laughs, but there's an edge to it. "You going to fight me, boy? Over some used-up piece of—"

I move before he can finish, my fist connecting with his jaw hard enough to snap his head back. The daisy falls from my other hand as pain shoots through my knuckles, but I barely notice.

"Don't you dare," I growl, advancing on him as he stumbles. "Don't you fucking dare talk about her like that."

The mist surges around us, and I swear the temperature drops several degrees. Phil's eyes widen slightly as he rights himself, blood trickling from his split lip.

"You don't know what you're dealing with," he spits, but there's fear creeping into his voice now. "Her father—"

"Isn't here." I cut him off, my voice carrying steel. "But I am. And if you ever come near her again..."

I let the threat hang, watching as he weighs his options. Behind me, I can hear Bree's ragged breathing, feel the way the mist coils protectively around both of us.

Phil's gaze darts past me to Bree, then back. Something calculating crosses his face before he takes a step back, raising his hands in mock surrender.

"Have it your way," he says, his smirk returning though it doesn't reach his eyes. "But this isn't over. Not by a long shot."

"It is for now." I don't move from my defensive stance, my body humming with adrenaline and barely contained violence.

Phil backs away slowly, his gaze never leaving us until he reaches the cemetery gates.

A long silence. Just the wind through the trees. Just the sound of Bree's ragged breathing.

Only when he disappears from view do I let my shoulders drop, turning to face Bree.

She stands frozen, her face pale in the morning light, arms wrapped tight around herself like she's trying to hold something in. Or keep something out.

"Bree," I start, softer now, but she shakes her head.

"Don't." Her voice trembles. "Just... don't."

The mist swirls between us, and I notice the daisy on the ground, still glowing faintly. When I reach for it, the petals pulse once, like a heartbeat.

In the distance, I hear car doors slam. Gray. The others. But I don't take my eyes off Bree, afraid she'll disappear again if I look away for even a second.

"I don't know what you heard last night," I say quietly. "But whatever you're thinking—"

"Stop." She takes another step back, her shoulders hunching like she's bracing for a blow. "You can't... I can't do this. Not with you. Not with any of you."

"Do what?" The words come out rougher than I mean them to, frustration bleeding through. "Trust us? Let us help you?"

Her laugh is bitter, broken. "Help me? Is that what you call it?"

"Bree—"

"He's right, you know." Her voice cracks around the edges. "About what people want from me. What they think I'm worth."

The fury that had cooled surges back, hot and sharp. "He's not right about anything."

"Isn't he?" Her eyes meet mine finally, bright with unshed tears. "I heard you. All of you. Talking about me like I'm something to be—"

She cuts off as footsteps approach, her gaze darting toward the sound. Gray appears first, moving with that predatory grace of his, followed by Theo, Wes and Jace. The mist thickens, almost solid now in its intensity.

"Don't," she whispers, but I'm not sure if she's talking to me or the mist or herself. "Please, just... let me go."

"We can't do that," Gray says quietly, stopping a few feet away. "Not this time."

Something flashes across her face—pain or fear or something deeper—before her walls slam back up. The mist surges around her, and for a moment, I swear it glows with the same light as the daisy still clutched in my hand.

"You don't get to decide that," she says, her voice steadier now but hollow. Empty. "None of you do."

Then she turns and runs, disappearing into the maze of headstones before any of us can move.

The mist surges with her, thick and consuming, swallowing her whole in a matter of seconds.

By the time we move, she's already gone

"Damn it," Jace mutters, already starting after her, but Gray catches his arm.

"Let her go."

"Are you kidding?" Jace tries to pull free, but Gray's grip doesn't loosen. "After what just happened? After Phil—"

"She needs space," Theo cuts in, his analytical tone barely masking his own worry. "We push now, we'll lose her completely."

I stare at the spot where she disappeared, the daisy still pulsing faintly in my palm. "We're already losing her."

No one argues. Because what can we say? That we didn't mean for her to hear us? That we were trying to protect her? That everything we've done—every careful word, every gentle touch, every moment of holding back—was because we thought we were doing the right thing?

The morning sun feels too bright, too harsh against the weathered stones around us. Against the fresh dirt of Mrs. Henderson's grave where we found her.

Where she was hiding from us.

"What do we do now?" Jace asks, his voice smaller than I've ever heard it.

I close my fingers around the daisy, feeling its warmth pulse against my skin like a reminder. Like a promise.

"We wait," I say finally. "And we hope she finds her way back."

But as the mist fades into the morning light, I can't help wondering if we've already lost our chance to make this right.

# Chapter 37
## UNKNOWN

*Fuck.*

Her pain hits hard, echoing across the veil between realms. The mist writhes around me, agitated and cold, carrying fragments of her despair.

This is not how it was supposed to happen.

I pace the length of my chamber, shadows dancing at my feet as her emotions surge through our connection. Fear. Betrayal. That bone-deep certainty that she's worth nothing more than what others would take from her.

*No, little flame. You're worth so much more.*

But she can't hear me. Not yet. And her guardians—those five souls who've loved her longer than they realize—they're fumbling in the dark, trying to protect her while unknowingly pushing her further away.

The mirror ripples as I press my palm against it, its surface shimmering like disturbed water. Through it, I catch glimpses: Rhett's bloody knuckles, the daisy pulsing with power he doesn't understand. Gray's calculated fury as he holds the others back, knowing they can't chase her. Not this time.

They don't realize what's at stake. How close she is to breaking completely.

Phil's words have cut deep, reopening old scars, making her doubt even those who truly love her. But it's not just manipulation—it's preparation. He isn't lying about her father. He's working for him. He's always been working for him."

"And she has no idea what that truly means.

The mist surges, and for a moment I see her through its eyes: running through the cemetery, tears she won't let fall burning in her eyes. The crown's mark burns beneath my skin in response, a sharp reminder of everything that's yet to come.

"Run if you must, little flame," I murmur to the empty air. "But remember—some bonds can't be broken. Not even by fear."

The mist coils tighter, carrying the echo of her heartbeat. Of their worry. Of destiny slowly, inexorably, pulling them all toward what they're meant to become.

*Together.*

If only they knew.

# Chapter 38
## THEO

The cemetery is too quiet in the wake of Bree's departure. Gray still has a firm grip on Jace's arm, though the fight has drained from both of them. The mist lingers at our feet, restless and cold, like it's as torn as we are between chasing her and letting her go.

"She heard us wrong," Jace says, his voice rough. "In the attic. She must have—"

"She heard exactly what she expected to hear," I cut in, the words tasting bitter. "What she's been conditioned to expect."

Movement catches my eye - Rhett, still staring at the daisy in his palm. It pulses faintly, the glow matching the rhythm of the mist swirling around us. Something about the sight tugs at my memory, like a half-remembered dream.

*We've been here before.*

The thought comes unbidden, nonsensical. But it settles in my chest with a weight that feels somehow familiar.

"She's going back to her apartment," Gray says, finally releasing Jace. His sharp eyes scan the horizon where Bree disappeared, calculating. "It's what she knows."

"It's not safe," Wes says quietly. He stands slightly apart from us, his dark eyes focused on something distant. "Not with Phil—"

"Phil's the least of our concerns right now," I say, though the words feel wrong even as they leave my mouth. Like I'm missing something crucial. "She thinks we see her the way he does. The way her father does."

Rhett's fingers close around the daisy, and I swear the temperature drops several degrees. "We have to fix this."

"How?" Jace demands, running a hand through his hair. "She won't even look at us. Won't let us explain—"

"Then we don't explain," Gray cuts in, his voice carrying that edge of steel it gets when he's found a solution none of us will like. "We show her."

The mist shifts, coiling around our feet in a pattern that makes my head spin. For a moment, just a breath, it forms shapes that look almost like crowns before dissolving back into formless vapor.

"Show her what?" Wes asks, but there's something in his tone that suggests he already knows.

"Everything," Gray says simply. "No more holding back. No more careful distance. We show her exactly what she means to us."

The words resonate through me like a bell being struck, stirring something that feels older than memory. My hands tingle with phantom sensation, like they remember touching something ancient and powerful.

"She'll run," Jace warns, but he doesn't sound convinced.

"She's already running," I point out, my analytical mind racing ahead even as that strange feeling of déjà vu persists. "At least this way she'll know what she's running from."

Rhett finally looks up from the daisy, his green eyes burning with something that makes my breath catch. "Or what she's running to."

The mist surges around us, and for a heartbeat, I see... something. Colors that shouldn't exist, power that feels as natural as breathing. Then it's gone, leaving only the certainty that we're standing on the edge of something vast and inevitable.

"We find her first," Gray says, already moving toward his truck. "Then we deal with Phil."

"And her father?" Wes asks, falling into step beside him.

Gray's jaw tightens. "One battle at a time."

But as we follow him out of the cemetery, that feeling of recognition lingers. Like we've fought this battle before, in another time, another place. Like we've always been meant to find our way back to her.

The daisy in Rhett's hand pulses once more, bright enough to cast shadows, before fading to a steady glow. None of us mention it. None of us have to.

Some things don't need words to be understood.

Some bonds don't need explanation to be felt.

# Chapter 39
## JACE

The key ring feels heavy in my pocket as I pace the sidewalk outside Bree's building. All those keys, given to us "for emergencies." Each one a sign of trust that we've somehow broken.

Gray's words echo in my head from our hasty planning session: *"No confrontation. No pushing. Just make sure she's safe."*

Easy for him to say. He's not the one watching her slip past with her head down, shoulders hunched, looking right through me like I'm not even here. At least we'd managed to time the shift changes with her work schedule. Small mercies.

Three days of this. Of waiting. Watching. Taking turns standing guard while trying to look like we're not standing guard. My usual charm feels useless here - there's nothing funny about the way she flinches when she sees us, nothing lighthearted about the shadows under her eyes.

Movement catches my attention - Mrs. Chen from 2B, giving me that suspicious look again as she waters her window plants. I flash my most winning smile, the one that usually gets me out of trouble.

"Beautiful morning for gardening," I call up, ignoring how my voice carries a bit too much forced cheer.

She mutters something that sounds distinctly unimpressed before disappearing back inside. Can't blame her. I probably look suspicious as hell, pacing the same stretch of sidewalk for hours.

"Real smooth."

I turn to find Theo approaching, coffee in hand. My relief must show because he smirks slightly as he passes me one of the cups.

"You're early," I say, though I'm grateful for both the caffeine and the company.

"Couldn't sleep." He leans against the wall, his sharp eyes scanning the street with practiced ease. "Any movement?"

"Light's been on since four." I try to keep my tone casual, like I haven't memorized every flicker of her window. "She's getting ready for her shift."

Theo nods, taking a slow sip of his coffee. Neither of us mentions how we've all got her schedule memorized now. How we've arranged our lives around making sure someone's always here, always watching.

The mist drifts lazily around our feet, thicker than usual this morning. It's been doing that more lately - gathering around the building like it's trying to shield her. Or maybe trying to tell us something we're too dense to understand.

"You seen Phil?" Theo asks quietly.

"Not since yesterday." My fingers curl into a fist at the memory. "Rhett's warning must have stuck."

"Or he's just getting smarter about hiding."

Before I can respond, the front door opens. Bree steps out, already in her scrubs, her dark hair pulled back in a messy bun. She freezes when she sees us both, something flashing across her face too quick to read.

"Morning," I try, keeping my voice light. Careful. "Beautiful day for a walk to work."

She doesn't answer, just pulls her bag closer to her chest and starts walking. I fall into step a few paces behind her, giving her space while staying close enough to intervene if needed. Theo hangs back, probably heading up to take his shift watching the building.

The silence stretches between us, heavy with all the things I want to say. *We love you. We'd never hurt you. Please come home.*

Because that's the thing - we do love her. We're in love with her. All of us. And we have been since the moment we laid eyes on her. It wasn't something that grew. It was a knowing. A bone-deep knowledge that she was ours and we were hers. We were just too stupid to admit it.

But I don't say any of it. I just walk, counting the cracks in the sidewalk, watching how the mist seems to follow her like a loyal pet. Three blocks to Maple Grove. Another day of standing guard while she takes care of others and ignores herself.

"You don't have to do this," she says suddenly, her voice barely above a whisper.

"Yes, we do." The words come out fiercer than I mean them to.

She doesn't respond, just walks faster. I match her pace easily, my longer stride keeping up without effort. The mist swirls around our feet, and for a moment - just a breath - I swear it forms patterns I almost recognize.

*We've always protected her*, something whispers in the back of my mind. The thought feels both foreign and achingly familiar, like a half-remembered song.

I shake it off as we approach Maple Grove. Bree pauses at the entrance, her hand tight around the strap of her bag.

"I'm safe here," she says, still not looking at me. "You can go."

"I'll be around." I try for casual but probably miss by a mile. "You know, if you need anything."

She doesn't answer, just disappears inside without a backward glance. I find my usual spot - the coffee shop across the street with the perfect view of both entrances. The barista knows my order by now, knows to keep the refills coming.

My phone buzzes - the group chat we've set up for exactly this.

Gray: *Status?*

Jace: *At work. No signs of Phil.*

Rhett: *Taking next shift. Update if anything changes.*

I pocket the phone, settling in for another long day of watching and waiting. The mist lingers outside Maple Grove's entrance, thick enough that other people seem to unconsciously step around it.

Some part of me knows we can't keep this up forever. That eventually something has to give.

I just pray it's not her.

# Chapter 40
## BREE

The day shift drags, each minute stretching like taffy as I move through my rounds. My hands work on autopilot—checking vitals, changing sheets, administering meds. Mrs. Peterson needs help with her lunch. Mr. Roberts keeps asking for Erin, though she transferred months ago.

I feel Jace's presence across the street like a physical weight. He thinks I don't notice him in that coffee shop, nursing endless refills while pretending to work on his laptop. Just like I pretend not to see Gray's truck idling at the corner during shift changes, or Theo's careful distance as he walks the perimeter.

The mist follows me through the halls, thicker than usual, curling around my ankles with an urgency I've never felt before. Like it's trying to warn me about something.

I shake it off, pushing through my exhaustion as I grab an empty linen cart and head toward the storage room. Fresh sheets, pillowcases, supplies—something to keep my hands busy, to keep my thoughts from spiraling.

The fluorescent lights flicker slightly as I step inside, the cool air a contrast to the warmth of the main hall. The mist lingers in the doorway, hesitant, curling back like it doesn't want to follow me in.

A prickle of unease crawls up my spine.

And then—

"Well, look who it is."

My heart slams against my ribs at the familiar voice. I turn slowly, already knowing what I'll find.

Phil stands in the doorway of the supply room, his bulk filling the space in a way that makes my skin crawl. His eyes are glassy, that dangerous kind of drunk that makes men think they're invincible.

"You can't be in here," I say, proud of how steady my voice sounds. "This is a restricted area."

He grins, showing too many teeth. "Funny thing about restricted areas - they're real good for private conversations."

The mist surges around my feet, colder than ice, as Phil takes a step forward. Another step. My back hits the shelves, supplies rattling behind me.

"Your daddy says hi," he slurs, close enough now that I can smell the whiskey on his breath. "Says you've been avoiding his calls. That's not very nice, princess."

The old nickname hits like a slap. My father's voice echoes in my head: *Come here, princess. Daddy needs you.*

"Get out." The words scrape out of my throat as the mist rises higher, coiling around my wrists like living smoke.

Phil's hand shoots out, grabbing my throat and slamming me against the shelves. Supplies crash around us as he presses closer, his other hand sliding down my side with sickening purpose.

"Finally," he growls, his eyes shifting to an unnatural silver. "Your father always called you princess didn't he. Almost fitting, isn't it?"

The pet name hits like a trigger. My father's voice echoes: *Show daddy what you can do, Princess.*

Something inside me snaps.

The mist explodes outward, but Phil doesn't stagger back in fear. He laughs - a harsh, grating sound as ice crystals form where the mist touches him. His grip tightens on my throat as power surges through me, ancient and familiar and terrifying.

"That's it," he hisses, his accent shifting to something older, something not of this world. "Let it out. Let me taste that power."

His free hand glows with sickly green light as he reaches for my chest, right where my heart pounds against my ribs. The mist writhes, recoiling like it can sense something is wrong.

Pain. Not from him, but from inside me. A sharp pressure behind my ribs, a weight that wasn't there before.

Phil smiles. "Yes, there it is," he breathes, his fingers inches away—

The mist erupts before he can touch me.

This time when the mist strikes, it's not just cold - it's a wave of pure force that tears Phil away from me. He hits the wall but lands gracefully, that unnatural silver gleam in his eyes growing brighter.

"Well done," he says, straightening his shirt with inhuman calm. "Your father will be pleased to know the binding is finally breaking. Though he may not appreciate how I... accelerated the process."

The word hits like a trigger, and the mist surges again. This time when it strikes, Phil flies backward, slamming into the wall hard enough to knock the breath from his lungs. He crumples, wheezing, as frost spreads across the floor in intricate patterns.

I stare at my hands, at the mist swirling between my fingers like it belongs there. Like it's always belonged there. This isn't like before - this isn't just the mist reacting. This is me. This is power I can feel thrumming under my skin, that's somehow familiar and completely terrifying.

Footsteps pound down the hall - Jace, bursting through the door with Theo right behind him. Their expressions shift from panic to something darker as they take in the scene: the upended supplies, the frost still crystallizing in the air, the mist coiling around me like a storm.

"Bree." Jace's voice catches as he starts forward, but Phil's laugh stops him cold.

"Perfect timing," Phil says, that unnatural silver still gleaming in his eyes. "Make sure she doesn't try to run. She'll need her strength for what's coming."

"The only thing coming is me breaking your jaw," Jace snarls, but Phil just smiles - that same cruel twist of lips that haunts my nightmares.

"Such loyal dogs," he says, his accent still carrying that strange, otherworldly lilt. "Always circling, always protecting. But you don't even know what you're protecting her from, do you?"

Theo moves with fluid grace, positioning himself between Phil and me. "Leave. Now."

Phil straightens his collar, utterly calm despite the ice still clinging to his skin. "My work here is done anyway," he says smoothly. His gaze lingers on me, and for the first time, I realize he's not afraid. Not at all.

"It won't be long now, princess. When you wake up... you'll understand everything."

He turns and walks away - not stumbling, not fleeing, but moving with deliberate purpose. Like everything that just happened was exactly according to plan.

My legs give out. The mist catches me before I hit the ground, but Jace is there too, his hands hovering near but not touching as I slide down the wall.

"I've got you," he murmurs, and for once I don't have the strength to pull away. "You're safe. We've got you."

But I'm not safe. I'll never be safe. The power that surged through me moments ago leaves me hollow, drained. I stare at my hands, still expecting to see frost or silver light or something to explain what just happened.

"The mist," I whisper, my voice raw. "It wasn't just... it was me. I did that."

"We know," Theo says quietly, crouching beside us. His calculated calm cracks slightly as he looks at the bruises forming on my throat. "We've always known there was something different about the way it responds to you."

"Different?" A hysterical laugh bubbles up. "I nearly froze him solid. I'm a freak. A monster. Just like he-"

"Stop." Jace's voice carries an edge I've never heard before. "You're not a freak. You're not a monster. You're..."

He trails off, and something flickers across his face - confusion, recognition, gone too fast to read. The mist drifts between us, gentler now but still active, still mine in a way I can't deny anymore.

"We need to get her out of here," Theo says, his tone shifting back to analytical. "Before someone comes looking."

"My shift," I start, but Jace shakes his head.

"Sarah's already covering for you. Called in a family emergency." His lips twist. "Technically not even a lie."

Family. The word hits harder than it should. Phil's voice echoes in my head: *Your father will be pleased...*

"I can't go back there," I whisper, and they both know I don't mean the house. I mean everything - the life I had, the person I thought I was. "I don't even know what I am anymore."

"You're Bree," Jace says firmly. "You're ours. The rest... the rest we figure out together."

The mist curls around all three of us now, and for a moment - just a breath - I swear I see something in Jace's eyes. The way he looks at me like I'm more than I know. It doesn't take away the fear, but it calms it for at least a few moments.

# Chapter 41
## GRAY

My phone buzzes against the dash. Theo's name lights up the screen, and something in my chest goes cold before I even answer.

"We're coming," is all he says. His voice carries that careful control that means everything's wrong. "Pull up front."

I'm already moving before he hangs up, the truck's engine roaring to life. Three days of watching, of waiting, and still we weren't fast enough. My knuckles whiten on the steering wheel as I swing around to the entrance.

The sight of Bree cradled in Jace's arms makes my blood run cold. She looks small, fragile in a way she'd hate if she was conscious to notice. Frost clings to her scrubs, delicate patterns that shouldn't be possible in this heat.

Theo opens the back door before I can move, helping Jace maneuver her inside. "Home," he says quietly, and I catch the weight in that single word. Not her apartment. Home.

"What happened?" I ask as we pull away, watching them in the rearview. Bree's head rests in Jace's lap, his fingers hovering near but not touching, like he's afraid she'll shatter.

"Phil." Theo's voice carries barely controlled rage. "He was waiting. But Gray..." He pauses, choosing his words carefully. "The mist. It wasn't just reacting this time. She controlled it."

"Controlled it?"

"Phil was on the ground when we got there," Jace says, his voice rough. "Ice everywhere. The mist—I've never seen it like that before. And his eyes..." He trails off, something flickering across his face that looks almost like recognition.

"Silver," Theo finishes. "Inhuman. He wasn't surprised either." He hesitates, glancing at Jace. "You said he mentioned something about a binding breaking?"

Jace nods, his jaw tight. "Yeah. Like it was inevitable. Like he'd been waiting for it."

A heavy silence settles between us, the weight of those words pressing down like a storm on the horizon.

My grip tightens on the wheel as pieces click into place. The mist's increasing activity. The way Phil's been watching her. Her father's shadow lurking behind everything.

"The others?" I ask.

"Already called them." Theo types something on his phone. "They're meeting us at home. Wes is bringing supplies - medical kit, just in case."

"Rhett?"

"Making sure Phil doesn't follow."

I nod, understanding everything Theo isn't saying. Rhett's rage needs direction right now, and following Phil is better than the alternative.

The house comes into view, and something in my chest eases at the sight of Wes's car already in the drive. The porch light glows warm against the growing dusk, and I catch movement behind the curtains - the others preparing.

"We moved her things," I say as I park, glancing at Theo. "While you were on watch. The attic..."

"Good." He nods, already moving to help Jace. "She needs somewhere that feels safe. Really safe."

I lead the way, unlocking the door as Jace carries her inside. The mist follows, curling around our feet like it's making sure we're taking her somewhere secure. Wes appears at the top of the stairs, his dark eyes taking in everything - the frost on her clothes, the bruises forming on her throat, the way Jace holds her like she's precious.

The attic feels different as we climb the stairs - warmer, lived-in. We'd worked in shifts while she was gone, the ones not on guard duty throwing themselves into making this space truly hers. Her books line the shelves now, arranged the way she always kept them. The bed we'd built is piled with soft things in shades of green and blue. Little touches everywhere - the reading lamp she'd mentioned liking, the throw blankets she always gravitates toward, her journal on the window seat where she can watch the daisies.

Jace settles her on the bed with careful movements while Wes sets up the medical supplies. None of us speak - we don't need to. We move around each other with practiced ease, each knowing our role in this dance we've been performing since childhood.

"Her pulse is steady," Wes says quietly, his fingers gentle on her wrist. "Temperature's low, but..."

"The ice," Theo supplies. "The power she used - it drained her."

I watch from the doorway as they work, cataloging every detail. The way the mist seems to approve of the space, drifting contentedly around the room. How Bree's breathing evens out, some of the tension leaving her face as she settles into the bed we made for her. The careful distance we all maintain while still staying close enough to protect.

"She'll have questions," Jace says finally, running a hand through his hair. "When she wakes up."

"We all do," I reply, but my eyes stay on Bree. On the girl we've loved since before we understood what love was. On the power that's breaking free.

The mist swirls lazily around us, and for a moment - just a breath - I swear I feel something. A memory, maybe. Or an echo of one. But then it's gone, leaving only the certainty that everything is about to change.

We settle in to wait - Jace by the window, Theo near the door, Wes checking her vitals with careful precision. And me, watching it all, trying to piece together a puzzle that feels bigger than any of us realized.

When Rhett joins us later, fury still simmering beneath his controlled movements, none of us mention the blood on his knuckles. Some questions can wait.

For now, we guard her sleep and pray that when she wakes, she'll finally let us explain that she's not alone. That she's never been alone.

And she never will be again. For as long as she'll have us.

# Chapter 42
## BREE

*I'm falling, drowning in a sea of memories that aren't mine, yet are undeniably a part of me. The dream grips me, pulling me deeper into a past I've never known but feel in my bones.*

*Phil's face looms before me, twisted with a cruel hunger that makes my skin crawl. His fingers dig into my flesh, and I can feel him reaching inside me, grasping at something intangible yet vital. My power. My essence. It flows through my veins like starlight, and he's determined to drain every last drop.*

*Fire comes first, ripped from my core in a blaze of agony. I scream, my voice echoing in this dreamscape that feels all too real. The flames that once danced at my fingertips sputter and die, leaving me cold and diminished.*

*Ice follows, crackling as it's torn away. The frost that used to coat my thoughts, giving me clarity and precision, melts into nothingness. I'm left raw and exposed, my mind a jumble of fractured thoughts.*

*Air rushes out of me next, leaving me gasping and weak. The currents I once commanded abandon me, and I'm left earthbound and heavy.*

*Water flows from my eyes, not just tears but the very essence of the tides I used to control. It streams down my face, pooling at my feet before vanishing into shadow.*

*The shadows themselves are torn away last - my darkness, my ability to hide and protect myself. Phil pulls them from me like threads unraveling from a tapestry, each one taking a piece of me with it.*

*But even as he strips away every power he can find, the mist remains - so subtle, so intertwined with my soul that he doesn't recognize it as power at all. It curls through me, around me, holding the fragments of myself together even as everything else is taken.*

*The pain is beyond anything I could have imagined. It's not just physical; it's a soul-deep ache that threatens to unmake me entirely. But even as I crumble, even as Phil's laughter rings in my ears and his hands continue their vicious work, I cling to a single thought.*

*I'm doing this for them. My men. Wes, with his steady strength. Rhett, fierce and loyal. Gray, whose quiet intensity anchors me. Theo, brilliant and passionate. Jace, wild and free. And Thane.*

*Their faces flash before me, a kaleidoscope of love and devotion. I hold onto these images as Phil continues his torture, reminding myself that this sacrifice is worth it. For them, I would endure a thousand lifetimes of pain.*

*But even as I try to stay strong, I can feel myself slipping away. With each power Phil strips from me, a piece of my identity goes with it. I'm losing myself, becoming less and less with each passing moment.*

*The dream shifts, blurring at the edges. I'm no longer just experiencing the torture; I'm watching it happen to a version of myself I barely recognize. She's on her knees, head bowed, while Phil towers over her. The air around them crackles with stolen power, and I want to scream, to fight, to do something to stop this.*

*The dream shifts again, flickering between memory and nightmare. The mist coils tighter, shielding me from Phil's grasp. But his voice—his voice follows me into the dark."*

"See you soon, princess."

I wake up gasping.

Cold. Everything feels cold.

Consciousness returns in fragments, like shards of ice melting slowly. The first thing I register is softness beneath me, different from my lumpy couch at home. Then voices, low and careful, filtering through the fog in my head.

"Her temperature's still low," someone murmurs. Wes, I think. His voice carries that quiet steadiness I'd know anywhere.

"The frost is finally melting though." Theo this time, analytical even in his concern.

Frost? The word catches in my mind, tugging at memories that feel sharp and jagged. Phil's face, twisted with something inhuman. The mist surging around me, cold and fierce. Power flowing through my veins like liquid ice.

I try to open my eyes, but they feel heavy. My whole body aches, like I've been running for hours. The mist curls around me - I can feel it even with my eyes closed, its presence somehow warmer than usual, almost protective.

"She's waking up." Gray's voice, closer than the others. "Give her space."

My fingers twitch against what feels like a blanket - softer than anything I own. The scent of cedar and pine fills my lungs, familiar and grounding. When I finally manage to pry my eyes open, the first thing I see is the attic ceiling, its exposed beams bathed in soft light.

The attic. They brought me to the attic.

"Easy," Rhett says as I try to sit up. His hand hovers near my shoulder but doesn't touch, giving me the choice. "You've been out for a while."

My throat feels raw when I try to speak. "What..." I swallow and try again. "What happened?"

The guys exchange glances - five sets of eyes carrying weights I can't quite read. The mist swirls thicker around the bed, and for a moment, I swear it pulses in rhythm with my heartbeat.

"What do you remember?" Theo asks carefully, his blue eyes sharp with that focused concern that means he's cataloging every detail.

The dream crashes back - powers being stripped away, a version of me I don't recognize, Phil's cruel laughter. I shudder, trying to separate nightmare from reality. "I... there was ice. The mist... it listened to me. And Phil, he..."

My hands find my way to my neck, my voice breaks as more recent memories surface: Phil's grip on my throat, the sour stench of his breath, the way his eyes changed when the mist responded to my fear. Then... power. Ice crystals forming in the air, the mist becoming solid enough to throw him across the room.

"I..." My voice cracks. "Did I...?"

"Yeah," Jace says softly from his perch by the window. "You did."

The confirmation hits harder than I expect. My hands shake as I press them flat against the blanket, trying to ground myself. Ice shouldn't be possible. The mist shouldn't be able to... I shouldn't be able to...

"Breathe," Gray commands quietly, and I realize I'm starting to hyperventilate. "You're safe here."

But am I? The thought spirals as I look around the attic - at the careful way they've arranged themselves around me, at the medical supplies on the bedside table, at the frost still clinging to my scrubs.

"Phil," I manage, the name tasting like ash on my tongue. "He said something about... a binding breaking?"

Rhett's jaw tightens, and I notice for the first time the bruises on his knuckles. What did he do after I passed out?

"We'll figure it out," Wes says, his dark eyes steady when I meet them. "Together."

The word settles over me like another blanket - heavy but not suffocating. The mist drifts closer, curling around my fingers where they grip the covers. Its touch feels different now, more deliberate. Like it's trying to tell me something.

"I'm not..." I stop, struggling to find the words. "This isn't normal."

"No," Gray agrees, his voice carrying that quiet certainty that both steadies and terrifies me. "But neither is the way the mist has always followed you. Or those daisies you planted."

I glance toward the window, where the faint glow of the flowers is visible even from here. They pulse softly in the growing dusk, like they're responding to my awareness of them.

"What am I?" The question slips out before I can stop it, small and afraid.

Five sets of eyes meet mine, and something in their combined gaze makes my chest tighten. There's no fear there, no judgment. Just fierce protection and something deeper - something that feels ancient and new all at once.

"You're ours," Rhett says simply, like it's the most obvious truth in the world. "The rest we'll figure out together."

The mist swirls higher, wrapping around all of us like it's sealing a promise I'm not sure I'm ready to make. But as I sit here, surrounded by their steady presence and the quiet magic humming through my veins, I let myself believe - just for a moment - that maybe I don't have to face this alone.

The dream lingers at the edges of my mind, a warning or a memory - I'm not sure which. But something tells me the answers are closer than I think, hidden in the mist that's followed me all my life, waiting to be remembered.

# Chapter 43
## BREE

The name echoes in my mind like a half-remembered song.

*Thane.*

It doesn't belong with my other memories - not the ones I know are real - and yet it feels as vital as breathing. As natural as the mist curling around my fingers.

"Who's Thane?" The question slips out before I can stop it.

The effect is immediate. Five heads snap toward me, their expressions shifting from protective concern to something sharper, more alert. The mist thickens, responding to the sudden tension in the room.

"What did you say?" Gray's voice is carefully neutral, but there's an edge to it I've never heard before.

I swallow hard, fighting the urge to take back the question. "In my dream, there was... a name. Thane." My fingers twist in the soft blanket. "It felt important."

Wes moves toward me, his dark eyes intent. "I've been trying to figure that out myself."

"What do you mean?" Theo asks, his analytical focus shifting to Wes.

"The name," Wes says quietly. "It's been... appearing. In dreams. Like something I should remember but can't quite grasp."

The mist swirls between us, heavier now, almost expectant. I catch movement near the mysterious door - a subtle shift in the shadows that draws my eye. For a moment, I swear I see something green in the crack beneath it, but when I blink, it's gone.

"You're having dreams too?" Jace asks, his usual playful demeanor stripped away. "Why didn't you say anything?"

"Because it didn't make sense," Wes replies, his gaze meeting mine. "Not until now."

Rhett shifts closer to the bed, his presence steady but thrumming with contained energy. "What else was in the dream, Bree?"

I close my eyes, trying to sort through the fragments. "Power. Phil was... taking it. Different kinds - fire, ice, air, water, shadow. But the mist..." I pause, remembering how it felt. "The mist stayed. Like he couldn't see it. Couldn't touch it."

"Like it was protecting you," Gray says softly. It's not a question.

I open my eyes to find him watching me with an intensity that should be frightening but somehow isn't. "Yes."

The room falls quiet, heavy with unspoken understanding. The mist drifts between us, connecting us in ways I'm only beginning to comprehend. My gaze is drawn again to the door, and this time I'm certain - there's something growing in the crack where it meets the floor. Something small and green and impossibly alive.

"The daisies," I whisper, more to myself than them. "They've always been there too, haven't they? Like the mist."

"They're different now," Theo observes, following my gaze to the window where the planted ones glow softly in the growing dusk. "Since you manifested your power."

"Everything's different," I say, but the words don't carry the fear they should. Instead, they feel like truth finally breaking free.

The mist pulses gently, wrapping around each of us like it's trying to tell us something. Like it's been trying to tell us something all along.

"We'll figure it out," Rhett says again, but this time when he reaches for my hand, I let him take it. His skin is warm against mine, grounding me in this moment that feels both strange and inevitable.

My eyes drift back to the door, to that hint of green pushing through impossible cracks. Something is changing. Something is growing.

And somehow, I know we're running out of time to understand what it all means.

A heavy silence settles over us, thick with unspoken thoughts. Then, as if unable to take the weight of it anymore, Jace pushes to his feet with a groan.

"Alright, enough doom and gloom. She needs food."

"I'm fine," I start, but Jace just raises an eyebrow. "Your stomach begs to differ, sweetheart."

Before I can argue, he stretches dramatically and heads for the stairs. "I'll grab something. If I leave it up to Theo, it'll be some sad protein bar and a lecture about nutritional balance."

"Excuse me," Theo deadpans, shifting from his spot near the bed. "I'll have you know my taste in literature is impeccable, and that's more important right now." He disappears for a moment before returning with a book, setting it down beside me. "Something to distract you."

Rhett stands next, grabbing an extra blanket from the chest and draping it over my legs without a word. I don't argue. His warmth lingers where the fabric settles, calming me more than I want to admit.

Gray stays near the door, his arms crossed, watching everything like he's expecting trouble. Wes stands beside the bed, steady and silent, his dark eyes taking in every detail.

A few minutes later, Jace reappears, balancing a bowl of what smells like his famous chicken soup. The others watch as he sets it down with a flourish, along with a plate of fresh bread and a bottle of water.

"I'm not an invalid," I protest, but my stomach betrays me with an audible growl.

"No one said you were," Theo responds calmly, setting the bowl on the small table beside the bed. "But after today…"

He doesn't finish the sentence. He doesn't have to. The weight of everything - the dreams, the name that shouldn't mean anything but does, the power growing inside me - sits heavy in the air between us.

"Fine," I sigh, accepting the bowl. The warmth seeps into my palms, grounding me in the moment. "But you don't all have to hover."

"We're not hovering," Jace says, dropping onto the floor with his usual dramatic flair. "We're keeping you company. Totally different thing."

Gray takes up position near the window, his sharp eyes scanning the darkening yard where the daisies still glow faintly. Rhett settles against the wall, close enough to reach if needed but giving me space. Wes remains near the door, quiet but present, while Theo perches on the edge of the bed with careful precision.

The soup is perfect - rich and comforting in a way that makes my chest ache. I can't remember the last time someone brought me food in bed, cared enough to make sure I ate. The thought threatens to overwhelm me, but I focus on each spoonful, on the quiet conversation flowing around me.

"Try the bread," Jace insists, breaking off a piece and passing it up. "I didn't even burn it this time."

"Miracle of miracles," Theo mutters, but there's fondness in his tone.

The mist drifts lazily around us, touching each of them in turn like it's making sure they're really here. Like it wants them to stay as much as part of me does.

When I finish eating, they show no signs of leaving. Jace sprawls on his back, launching into a story about his latest real estate disaster that has even Gray cracking a smile. Theo grabs a book, settling in like he plans to be here a while. Rhett and Wes exchange looks I can't quite read, but neither moves toward the door.

"You don't have to stay," I say finally, though my voice lacks conviction. The massive bed I'm in, its size suddenly making a strange sort of sense.

"We're not leaving," Rhett says simply, already settling onto the floor near the window. The others move with quiet purpose - Theo gathering extra blankets from the chest, Gray positioning himself near the door like a sentinel, Jace sprawling on his back with deliberate casualness that doesn't quite hide his watchfulness.

"This is ridiculous," I mutter, perched on the edge of the bed that could easily fit all of us. "You can't sleep on the floor."

"Watch us," Jace quips, though his usual playful tone carries an edge of something fiercer. Something protective.

Wes takes position near the headboard, his back against the wall, dark eyes steady. "Sleep, Bree. We'll be here."

But sleep feels impossible with them arranged around me like guardians, their presence both comforting and overwhelming. I pull my knees to my chest, watching as Theo methodically distributes blankets.

"At least take turns on the bed," I try again. "It's huge enough."

"We're fine where we are," Gray says quietly from his post.

I fall silent, knowing better than to argue when they get like this. Instead, I find myself studying them - the way Rhett's shoulders remain tense even as he settles, how Theo's fingers absently trace patterns in the air like he's puzzling something out, the steady rhythm of Wes's breathing beside me.

"Tell me about the dreams," I say softly, not sure who I'm asking.

Wes shifts slightly, his voice low but clear in the quiet room. "They're fragments mostly. Places I've never been but feel familiar. People I should know but can't quite see clearly." He pauses. "And always the mist, leading me somewhere."

"To a crown," I whisper, the memory sharp and sudden.

The mist thickens around us, and I swear the temperature drops just slightly. By the door, something green pushes through another crack, delicate but insistent.

"What do you think it means?" I ask, not expecting an answer.

"Maybe it means we're supposed to be here," Theo says thoughtfully. "All of us. Together."

The words settle over me with unexpected weight. I glance around at them - these five men who've been my protectors, my anchors, my family for as long as I can remember. The mist swirls between us, connecting us in ways I'm only beginning to understand.

"Together," I repeat softly, testing how the word feels. It should scare me, this closeness, this trust. But tonight, surrounded by them, it feels like coming home.

The conversation drifts, quiet words and shared silences, until exhaustion finally pulls me under. The last thing I remember is Wes's steady presence beside me, the others arranged like stars in their own constellation, and the mist holding us all in its gentle embrace.

For the first time in years, I sleep without nightmares.

# Chapter 44
## BREE

The house has settled into a comfortable quiet, the kind that only comes late at night when the world finally exhales. I lie in bed, staring at the ceiling, listening to the faint creaks and whispers of the old Victorian. The day passed in a blur of soft voices, warm meals, and too much attention I didn't feel like I deserved.

They insisted I stay in bed, taking shifts to check on me. Rhett brought me coffee, the same way he used to when I had to cram for finals. Jace cracked jokes at the door, trying to coax a smile out of me. Gray sat in the chair by the window with his usual sharp focus, acting like he wasn't watching every move I made. And Theo... Theo was steady, quiet, leaving a book on the nightstand without a word.

I've never felt so cared for. Or so smothered.

It's not their fault. They're just trying to help. But the weight of their concern presses against my chest, suffocating in its gentleness. I needed the rest, sure, but now I feel like I'm crawling out of my skin. The mist stirs faintly at the edges of the room, restless, like it's echoing my unease.

Sliding out of bed, I grab Rhett's hoodie from the chair and pull it on, the hem brushing against my thighs. The house feels cooler now, the warmth of the day fading into the stillness of night. My feet move without direction, carrying me down the hall like they know where I'm supposed to go before I do.

Light spills softly from the study, pooling in the hallway like a beacon. I pause just outside, drawn by the quiet hum of a turned page. Peeking in, I spot Theo, sitting in the oversized armchair with a book balanced on his knee. A single lamp casts a warm glow over him, highlighting the sharp angles of his face and the relaxed curve of his shoulders.

He doesn't look up, but I know he knows I'm here. It's Theo. He always knows.

"You're up late," he says, his voice low and even, like he's afraid to break the quiet.

"So are you." I step inside, the thick rug soft under my bare feet. "What are you reading?"

He tilts the book slightly so I can see the cover. It's one of the ones he left on my nightstand—a battered old paperback with a cracked spine. I recognize the title immediately, a rush of familiarity warming my chest.

"I read that in high school," I say, moving closer. "It's... good."

Theo raises an eyebrow, his lips twitching like he's fighting a smile. "That's high praise."

"I mean it." I hover by the arm of the chair, unsure if I should sit or leave. "It's one of those books that sticks with you. The kind you think about years later."

He nods, his dark eyes soft as they meet mine. "That's why I like it. It doesn't tell you what to feel—it just... lingers."

The silence between us feels gentle, not awkward, and I find myself sinking onto the edge of the ottoman near his feet. The mist curls faintly at the corners of the room, barely visible in the low light, but I can feel it—warmer, steadier.

"Why do you read so much?" The question slips out before I can stop it. "I mean, you were always reading. Even when we were kids."

Theo leans back in the chair, his gaze distant, like he's looking through the book to something beyond it. "It's quiet. Books don't ask for anything. They don't judge. They just... exist."

Something about his answer makes my throat tighten. I look down at my hands, fidgeting with the hem of Rhett's hoodie. "I think that's why I started reading. It felt... safer than the real world. Easier."

"Still feel that way?" he asks softly, and I can hear the careful weight in his question. He's not pushing—he never pushes. But he's giving me space to answer if I want to.

I shrug, staring at the grain of the wooden floor. "Sometimes. I mean, I like being here. With you guys. But it's... a lot. All at once."

Theo doesn't respond right away, but when I glance up, his expression is calm, patient. "It's okay to need space," he says after a moment. "We're not going anywhere."

The mist shifts slightly, swirling around his legs and brushing against my ankles. It feels softer somehow, curious rather than restless. I reach out absently, my fingers brushing against the edge of the ottoman where the mist lingers. It doesn't feel cold this time—it feels... alive.

Theo notices but doesn't comment. Instead, he closes the book, setting it gently on the armrest. "What about now?" he asks. "Does this feel like too much?"

"No." The word slips out before I can think. "This is... nice."

His lips curve into a faint smile, and for a moment, I forget how to breathe. He has that effect on me—always has, though I've never let myself dwell on it. It's the quiet steadiness of him, the way he holds himself like he's unshakable but never cold. The way his dark eyes seem to see past every wall I've built, straight to the pieces of me I'm still trying to figure out.

I know I should look away, should pull back before he notices the way my cheeks warm or the way my fingers curl against the edge of the ottoman to keep from fidgeting. But I can't. Because this—him—is different.

Theo doesn't overwhelm me like Jace's relentless charm or Gray's sharp intensity. He doesn't try to pull me out of my head the way Rhett does, or linger in the background like Wes. He's just here, present and solid, like he'll wait forever if that's what I need.

And maybe that's why it scares me. Why he scares me.

Because Theo makes me feel seen, even when I don't want to be. He makes me feel safe in a way I've never been able to trust, like he's the anchor I didn't realize I was drifting without. And it's terrifying, this quiet, steady pull toward him that feels like gravity.

It's not just that he's beautiful—though God, he is. The sharp angles of his jaw, the warmth in his eyes, the way his hair falls just slightly out of place like he's too focused on the world around him to care. It's everything he is beneath that. The patience, the kindness, the way he listens without judgment, without expecting anything in return.

Being near him feels like standing in the eye of a storm. Calm and quiet, even when everything else inside me is chaos. The silence stretches between us, but I'm not uncomfortable. Not scared. Just... here.

The mist swirls higher, wrapping faintly around Theo's wrist where it rests on the arm of the chair. He doesn't pull away, doesn't flinch. He just watches me with that steady, unshakable presence that's always made me feel like maybe I'm not as broken as I think I am.

Years of memories flood back - Theo sitting next to me in the library, never pushing, just being there. The way he'd leave books on my desk in high school when I was having a bad day. How he noticed which ones made me smile and somehow always found more like them. All those quiet moments when the world felt too heavy, and he'd just... appear. Like he knew.

My throat tightens. "I don't know how to do this," I whisper, the words barely audible.

"Do what?" His voice is soft, patient.

"Let someone see me." My fingers twist in the hem of Rhett's hoodie. "Really see me. All of it. The broken parts, the scared parts, the..." I swallow hard. "The parts that want to stay."

Theo stays perfectly still, but I can feel the weight of his attention like a physical thing. "You don't have to be whole to be worthy of being seen, Bree."

The words hit like a punch to the chest, stealing my breath. Because that's what I've been afraid of, isn't it? That if they - if he - saw all of me, the real me, they'd finally understand how damaged I am. How unfixable.

"I keep waiting," I say, my voice cracking, "for you all to realize I'm not worth this. Worth..." I gesture vaguely at the room, at the house, at everything they've given me. "Any of it."

"You've never been something to fix," Theo says quietly. "You're someone to protect. To cherish. To..." He pauses, and I can hear him choosing his words carefully. "To love."

Something breaks inside me - a wall I didn't even know was still standing. Tears spill over before I can stop them, hot and relentless. I try to turn away, to hide, but Theo's hand moves finally, catching mine where it trembles against the chair.

His touch is gentle, barely there, but it anchors me as the sobs I've been holding back for years tear free. All the pain, all the fear, all the longing I've never let myself feel - it crashes through me like a wave, threatening to pull me under.

But Theo's there, steady and sure, his fingers laced with mine as I fall apart.

# Chapter 45
## THEO

She breaks like something beautiful - all at once and then slowly, each tear carrying years of pain she's never let herself feel. Her small frame shakes with the force of it, and before I can think, before I can stop myself, I'm pulling her into my lap.

She comes willingly, curling into me like she belongs there. Like she's always belonged there. Her face presses into my neck, her tears hot against my skin, and my arms wrap around her on instinct.

"I've got you," I whisper into her hair, one hand cradling the back of her head. "I've always had you."

The mist swirls around us, warmer than I've ever felt it, almost protective in its intensity. It feels like approval. Like recognition. Like maybe it's been waiting for this moment as long as I have.

How many nights had I watched her from afar, seeing the weight she carried? How many times had I forced myself to stay back, to give her space when everything in me screamed to hold her like this? To tell her that she wasn't alone. That she never had been.

"I used to dream about this," I admit softly, my fingers threading through her hair. "Not the tears. But holding you. Being allowed to comfort you." I swallow hard, my own eyes burning. "Do you know how many times I heard you cry through those walls when we were kids? How many times I wanted to break down every door between us?"

She shudders against me, her fingers curling into my shirt. "Why didn't you?"

"Because you weren't ready." My voice cracks slightly. "And I would have waited forever if that's what you needed. I still would."

Her sobs quiet slightly, becoming something softer, more vulnerable. "I don't deserve this," she whispers against my neck. "Any of it. You. The others. This home you've built..."

"You deserve everything," I cut her off gently, my arms tightening around her. "Every bit of love we can give you. Every moment of peace. Every..." I pause, my heart pounding. "Every piece of my soul that's been yours since we were kids."

She goes still in my arms, her breath catching. For a moment, I think I've said too much, pushed too far. But then she presses closer, if that's even possible, her whole body melting into mine like she's finally letting go of something heavy she's been carrying.

"I'm scared," she whispers, her voice small but steady. "Of wanting this. Of wanting you. All of you."

My heart stutters at her words - at the admission I never thought I'd hear. "We're not going anywhere," I promise, pressing my lips to her temple. "Not me, not the others. We're here for as long as you'll have us."

The mist pulses gently around us, and I swear I feel it settle into my bones, connecting us in ways I'm only beginning to understand. Bree's tears have slowed, but she doesn't move away. If anything, she burrows closer, her body fitting against mine like she was made for this.

Made for us.

"Stay," she murmurs, the word barely audible. "Please."

"Always," I whisper back, and I mean it with every fiber of my being. "Always."

I hear Gray before I see him - that careful tread he uses when he's trying not to startle her. He appears in the doorway like a shadow, his sharp eyes taking in Bree curled in my lap, the way she trembles with quieting sobs. Something in his expression softens, and he moves into the room without a word, settling against the wall where she can see him if she chooses to look up.

Wes follows moments later, as if drawn by some invisible thread. His dark gaze meets mine over Bree's head, understanding passing between us. He claims the window seat, close enough to reach but giving her space.

The mist swirls thicker, warmer, as Rhett's broad frame fills the doorway next. His green eyes lock onto Bree's small form, and I see his hands clench at his sides - not with anger, but with the need to protect. To hold. He moves to sit on the floor near my feet, his shoulder brushing against my leg.

Jace is last, for once without his usual dramatic entrance. He just slips in quietly, finding a spot on the ottoman where Bree sat earlier. The five of us arrange ourselves around her like we've done it a thousand times, like we've always known exactly where we belong.

Bree's tears have slowed to occasional hiccups, but she doesn't pull away. If anything, she presses closer, her fingers still twisted in my shirt. The mist connects us all now, drifting between us like a physical manifestation of what we've always known but never said.

It's time. Time for truth. Time for her to understand that she wasn't hearing judgment that night, but devotion. Protection. Love.

I press my lips to her temple again, feeling her breath steady against my neck. "We're all here," I murmur. "If you want us to be."

She nods slightly, and I feel rather than hear her whispered "Yes."

# Chapter 46
## BREE

The tears have run dry, leaving me hollow but somehow lighter. I keep my face pressed against Theo's neck, his steady heartbeat anchoring me as I register the others' presence. They've arranged themselves around us like a constellation - each in their own space but connected, the mist drifting between them like stardust.

I should feel trapped. Overwhelmed. But their quiet strength wraps around me like a blanket, and for once, I let myself be held. Let myself be seen.

"I heard you," I whisper finally, my voice rough from crying. "That night in the attic. When Gray said..." I swallow hard, forcing the words out. "When he said I was something to be used and discarded."

The temperature in the room drops slightly as five bodies go rigid. The mist pulses, responding to their sudden tension.

"No." Gray's voice is sharp with something that sounds like pain. "God, Bree, no. That's not..." He exhales heavily. "I was talking about how your father and Phil saw you. How they treated you. It made me sick, knowing they'd made you feel worthless when you're..." He stops, his voice cracking. "When you're everything."

I lift my head slightly from Theo's shoulder, just enough to see Gray's face in the dim light. His usual sharp edges are softer now, raw with an emotion I've never let myself see before.

"We were angry," Wes says quietly from his spot by the window. "Angry that they hurt you. That they made you doubt your worth. That they made you think you had to run from us."

Jace leans forward, his usual playful demeanor stripped away. "You didn't hear the whole conversation, love. You didn't hear how we..." He runs a hand through his hair, frustrated. "How we've all been in love with you since we were kids."

The words hit something inside me, stealing my breath. I feel Theo's arms tighten around me, grounding me as my world tilts on its axis.

"What?" The word comes out barely audible.

"All of us," Rhett says from his spot near our feet. His green eyes burn with intensity as they meet mine. "Always you. Only you."

I shake my head, trying to make sense of what they're saying. "But that's not... you can't all..."

"Why not?" Theo's voice rumbles against my cheek where it's pressed to his chest. "Why can't we all love you? We already do."

The mist swirls higher, wrapping around each of them in turn before settling over us like a blanket. It feels different now - warmer, more alive. Like it's been waiting for this moment.

"I don't understand," I whisper, even as something deep inside me shifts, awakens. "How could you want... this?" I gesture vaguely at myself, at all my broken pieces.

"Because you're ours," Gray says simply, the words carrying the weight of years of certainty. "You always have been."

My fingers grip the hem of Rhett's hoodie, a bitter laugh escaping me. "You don't even know... haven't seen..." I take a shaky breath. "The scars. What he did to me. What they all did."

"We know," Wes says softly, his dark eyes intense. "We've always known."

"No." I shake my head against Theo's chest. "Not all of them. Not... not how ugly..."

"Stop." Gray's voice cuts through my spiral, firm but gentle. He moves from the wall, kneeling beside Theo's chair so he can meet my eyes. "Those scars? They're not ugly. They're proof you survived. Proof you're stronger than anyone I've ever known."

Theo's hand slides to my arm, his thumb brushing over the raised scar near my elbow - the one from the bottle. His touch is feather-light, reverent. "Every mark tells a story of what you overcame," he murmurs. "How could that ever be anything but beautiful?"

"I remember," Rhett says, his voice rough with emotion, "the day you got this one." His fingers ghost over my shoulder, where the jagged scar curves like a crescent moon. "You still came to my track meet. Sat in the bleachers even though I knew you were in pain. Because you promised you'd be there."

"You wore long sleeves in summer," Jace adds quietly, all his usual humor replaced with something deeper. "But sometimes, when you thought no one was looking, you'd roll them up. Like you were reminding yourself you were still here. Still fighting."

Tears blur my vision again as their words sink in. They've known. All this time, they've known and still...

"Every scar," Wes says, his quiet voice carrying in the stillness, "is a battle you won. Every mark is proof that you chose to live. To stay. Even when it would have been easier not to."

"We love all of you," Theo whispers against my hair. "Every scar. Every fear. Every piece you try to hide because you think it makes you unlovable." His arms tighten around me. "They make you *you*. And you're..."

"Perfect," Gray finishes, his green eyes fierce with conviction. "Not because you're unbroken. But because you're real. Because you're ours."

The mist pulses around us, warm and alive, as something inside me finally, finally breaks free. Not the jagged, painful kind of breaking - but like a bird taking flight, like chains falling away, like...

Like coming home.

"I don't know how to do this," I whisper, my voice rough from crying. "How to let myself have this. Have... all of you."

"You already do," Gray says softly from his spot against the wall. "You always have."

Theo's hand slides up my back, grounding me as I process their words. The genuine love in their eyes - not pity, not obligation, but real, steady love - makes my chest ache.

"Tell me," I say finally, forcing myself to be brave. "When did you know? That you..." I can't finish, but they understand.

"Third grade," Jace says immediately, a ghost of his usual grin touching his lips. "You punched Tommy Miller for making fun of my stutter. Stood there all fierce and tiny, daring anyone else to try something." His eyes soften. "That's when I knew you were it for me."

"The night of the storm," Wes adds quietly. "Senior year. The power went out and you showed up at my door with flashlights and that ratty blanket. Just sat with me until the thunder stopped." He looks down at his hands. "You knew I was afraid but never made me feel weak for it."

Rhett shifts slightly, his green eyes intense. "For me it was that night at the hospital, junior year. You'd been taking care of Mrs. Reynolds all week during your volunteer shifts, reading to her when no one else would visit. When she passed..." His voice softens. "You stayed with her. Held her hand so she wouldn't be alone. That's when I knew - your heart, your capacity to care even when it hurts... that's when I fell in love with you."

"For me it was gradual," Theo murmurs against my hair. "All those quiet moments in the library. The way you'd get lost in books, finding escape in stories. How you'd share the good parts with me, your eyes lighting up as you described them." His arms tighten slightly. "I fell in love with your soul piece by piece."

Gray is last, his sharp gaze holding mine. "I knew the first time I heard you crying through our shared wall. You were trying so hard to be quiet, to be strong." He swallows hard. "I knocked - three taps, remember? And you tapped back. That's when I knew I'd spend my life trying to protect you."

Tears slip down my cheeks again, but they feel different now. Lighter. Like finally letting go of something heavy I've been carrying.

"I don't..." I take a shaky breath. "I don't know if I can be what you all deserve."

"You already are," Wes says simply.

"Just by being you," Rhett adds softly.

"By surviving," Gray continues.

"By staying," Theo whispers.

"By letting us love you," Jace finishes.

The mist pulses around us, warm and alive, as something deep inside me finally, finally clicks into place. Like a key turning in a lock I didn't know existed. Like coming home to a place I've been searching for my whole life.

I'm not fixed. Not whole. Not yet. But here, surrounded by their steady love, their quiet strength, I feel something I've never let myself feel before.

Hope.

# Chapter 47
## BREE

The sky hasn't quite decided if it's dawn yet, the world caught in that soft blue moment between night and morning. I kneel in the damp grass, drawn to the daisies that seem to pulse with their own inner light. The glow is stronger now, almost mesmerizing in the pre-dawn stillness.

The mist curls around the flowers like it belongs there, warmer than I've ever felt it. After last night - after finally letting myself be seen, be held - everything feels different. Clearer somehow, like a veil has been lifted from my eyes.

I reach out, my fingers brushing one of the softly glowing petals. Heat spreads through my hand, not burning but alive, like touching sunlight made solid. The sensation travels up my arm, settling somewhere deep in my chest where all those broken pieces feel like they're slowly coming together.

"They're changing."

I don't startle at Gray's voice behind me. Maybe because the mist warned me he was there, or maybe because some part of me is finally learning not to fear gentle things.

He moves closer, his footsteps silent in the dewy grass, and crouches beside me. This close, I can smell the faint scent of coffee and motor oil that always clings to him, grounding and familiar.

The early morning light catches on Gray's sharp features as he studies the daisies, his usual intensity softened by something like wonder. The mist drifts between us, connecting rather than separating.

"They're not just glowing anymore," he says quietly. "They're... growing. Differently."

He's right. The stems have taken on an almost crystalline quality, delicate but strong, like glass spun from starlight. The petals shimmer with patterns I've never seen before - intricate swirls that remind me of the mark on the attic door.

"I don't understand what's happening," I admit, my voice barely above a whisper. "Any of it. The flowers, the mist, last night..."

Gray's hand settles in the grass near mine, not quite touching but close enough that I can feel his warmth. "Does it scare you?"

I consider lying, but after last night - after finally letting my walls crack - the truth slips out. "Not as much as it should."

His lips curve slightly, and the expression transforms his whole face. It's rare to see Gray smile, really smile, and something in my chest flutters at being the cause of it.

"The mist has always been different with you," he says, his voice thoughtful. "Even when we were kids. I used to watch it follow you around, respond to your moods. I thought I was imagining things."

"You could see it?" I turn to look at him fully, surprised. "I thought... I always tried to hide it. I thought I was crazy."

"We all saw it," he says simply. "We just didn't know how to talk about it. How to tell you that maybe you weren't the only one who felt its presence."

The mist swirls thicker between us, as if acknowledging his words. A tendril brushes my cheek, soft as a caress, before drifting to touch Gray's hand where it rests in the grass.

"After last night..." I start, then stop, unsure how to put into words how different everything feels. How the mist seems more alive, more purposeful. How my skin buzzes with something that feels like recognition, like waking up.

"After last night," Gray finishes for me, "you finally let yourself accept what's always been true." His sharp green eyes meet mine, intense but not overwhelming. "That you belong here. With us."

The daisies pulse brighter, their glow reflecting in Gray's eyes as he watches me. The mist weaves around us both now, and I swear I can feel his steady heartbeat through it, like we're connected by something older than memory.

"I'm not good at this," I whisper, though I'm not sure if I mean the magic or the intimacy or both.

"You don't have to be good at it." His hand moves finally, fingers brushing mine in the grass. "You just have to be willing to try."

The touch sends warmth spreading through my palm, up my arm, settling in that place in my chest that ached for so long. The daisies shimmer brighter, their crystalline stems chiming softly in the morning breeze.

And for the first time, I don't pull away.

The daisies chime, a sound like crystal wind chimes that shouldn't be possible from flowers. The noise draws attention - I hear the back door open, familiar footsteps crossing the dewy grass.

"That's new," Theo says softly, coming to stand behind us. His presence feels steady, grounding, after our night in the study.

Wes appears like a shadow at Gray's shoulder, his dark eyes fixed on the glowing flowers. The mist seems to reach for him, coiling around his ankles in greeting. Rhett and Jace aren't far behind, and suddenly we're all here, drawn to whatever's happening with these impossible blooms.

"They're not just glowing anymore," I say, echoing Gray's earlier observation. "They're changing. Growing into something... different."

As if responding to my words, the crystalline stems begin to pulse with light, sending waves of warmth through the ground beneath my knees. The patterns on the petals shift and swirl, forming and reforming into shapes that look familiar somehow.

"The door," Wes says suddenly, his quiet voice carrying in the still morning air. "The mark on the attic door - it's the same pattern."

He's right. The swirls match exactly what I traced on that strange door, the one that wouldn't open for any of them. The one that felt like it was waiting for something.

The mist thickens around us, no longer just drifting but moving with purpose. It weaves between us, connecting us all like a web of silver light. The sensation is different now - warmer, more alive. Like it's trying to tell us something.

"Bree," Rhett says, his voice low and careful. "Your hands."

I look down to find my fingers glowing faintly where they touch the grass near the daisies, the same shimmer as the flowers seeping into my skin. But it doesn't feel wrong or frightening. It feels... right. Like something clicking into place.

"The attic," I whisper, certainty flooding through me though I couldn't say why. "We need to go to the attic."

The attic feels different in the pre-dawn light, the space charged with something that makes my skin tingle. The guys follow me up silently, their presence steady at my back as I move toward the door that's haunted my thoughts since I first saw it.

The mist flows with us, thick and purposeful now, carrying the same warm energy as the daisies below. My fingers still shimmer faintly, and I can feel echoes of that crystalline chime vibrating in my chest.

"The mark," Wes murmurs, coming to stand beside me. "It's clearer now."

He's right. The strange symbol seems to pulse in the dim light, its flowing lines more defined than before. Like it's been waiting for this moment. For us.

"Can you feel it?" I ask softly, not sure how to explain the pull I feel, the way the air seems to thicken with possibility.

"Yes," Theo says from my other side, his quiet voice certain. "It's like..."

"Like coming home," Gray finishes, moving closer. His sharp eyes are focused on the door with an intensity that would normally make me nervous. But nothing about this feels wrong or frightening.

Rhett's warm presence settles behind me, close enough that I can feel his steady breathing. "We're here," he says simply, and I know he means more than just physically.

"Whatever happens," Jace adds, his usual playful tone replaced with something deeper, "we're not going anywhere."

The mist swirls around us all now, connecting us like stars in a constellation. I reach for the door, my still-shimmering fingers hovering near the mark that seems to call to something deep inside me.

"Together?" I whisper, though I'm not sure if I'm asking them or the mist or myself.

Five voices answer as one: "Together."

I press my palm against the symbol, and everything changes.

The mist surges, wrapping around us all in a cocoon of silver light. The mark beneath my fingers burns cold then hot, pulsing in time with my heartbeat - with all our heartbeats. Like six hearts finally beating as one.

Then the world goes white.

# Chapter 48
## UNKNOWN

The ether *screams.*

Not with pain - with recognition. With awakening. With the kind of joy that breaks worlds and remakes them anew.

I grip the edges of my scrying mirror, watching silver light explode through the mist that connects our realms. Centuries of waiting, of watching, of guiding her soul back to us again and again... and finally, *finally*, she remembers.

No. Not remembers. Not yet. But she's opening to it, to them, to the bond that's written in the very fabric of our existence. I can feel it in my bones, in the ether that flows through my veins - she's accepting what she is. What they are. What we've always been.

Their souls shine like beacons through the mist - five points of light surrounding her radiance. Even now, after all this time, they found their way back to her. As they always do. As they always will.

*Gray.* His soul burns sharp and bright, the shadow-walker who's guarded her through a thousand lifetimes.

*Rhett.* Steady as flame, his warrior's spirit unchanged by death and rebirth.

*Jace.* Light incarnate, his brilliance dimmed but never extinguished by the cycles of time.

*Wes.* Silent and deadly as winter's first frost, his devotion outlasting empires.

*Theo.* Knowledge seeker, dream weaver, his quiet power a perfect balance to her storm.

And her... *Gods*, but she glows. The ether surges around her like it's finally found its heart again, its queen, its reason for being. My fingers trace her image in the mirror, an echo of a touch I haven't been allowed in centuries.

"You're finding your way back," I whisper, watching the power build around them all. "You're finally letting yourself remember what it means to be loved by them. By all of us."

The mark on the door - my mark, *our* mark - pulses with ancient magic. Soon the crown that's waited so long will rest again upon her brow.

I press my palm flat against the mirror, feeling the ether respond to my touch. It yearns toward her, drawn by the magnetism of her awakening strength. The mirror ripples beneath my fingers as her power surges again, and for the first time in longer than I care to remember, I smile.

She's coming home to us. To all of us.

# Chapter 49
## BREE

The world spins back into focus slowly, like I'm surfacing from deep water. The attic looks different now, bathed in silver light that seems to pulse from the very walls. My palm still tingles where it pressed against the door's mark, and the guys' presence behind me feels like anchor points in a storm.

The mist swirls thick and purposeful around us all, no longer just following but *moving* with intent. It coils between us like liquid starlight, connecting us in ways I can't explain but somehow understand in my bones.

"Bree?" Theo's voice comes soft and steady from my left. "Are you okay?"

I nod, though 'okay' doesn't begin to cover what I'm feeling. Everything feels sharper, clearer, like I've spent my whole life looking through foggy glass and someone's finally wiped it clean.

"The door," Gray says, his usual sharp tone hushed with something like awe. "Look."

The mark beneath my palm pulses once, bright enough to cast shadows, then slowly begins to fade. In its place, lines of silver light spread like cracks in ice, tracing patterns across the dark wood that look familiar somehow. Like something from a dream I can't quite remember.

And there - pushing through the seams where door meets floor - those same crystalline daisies from the yard are growing, their stems impossibly strong as they wind upward. The green growth that started as just a hint days ago now blooms with purpose, trailing patterns of light that match the door's fading mark.

"I've seen this before," Wes murmurs, moving closer. His quiet presence steadies me as the door begins to hum beneath my touch. "In the mist, sometimes. When it shows me things..."

The daisies pulse in time with the vibration building in the door, their crystalline stems chiming that impossible sound we heard in the yard. Not violent but insistent, like they're trying to help reveal what the door's been keeping safe all this time.

Rhett's hand settles on my shoulder, warm and grounding. "Together," he reminds me softly, echoing our earlier promise.

"Always," Jace adds from my right, his usual playful tone stripped to something raw and honest.

The mist surges around us, and this time I don't fight it. I let it flow through me, around me, connecting us all like stars in a constellation I'm only now beginning to see. The door shimmers, and I feel something *click* - not in the wood, but deeper. Like a key turning in a lock I didn't know I carried.

The door swings open.

Silver light spills out, but it's different from the mist. Older. Wilder. The room beyond shouldn't exist - the attic isn't big enough to hold this space that feels endless and intimate all at once. Ancient stones line walls that pulse with their own inner light, and in the center...

"Oh," I breathe, the sound barely a whisper.

The crown hovers in a column of light, delicate and devastating in its beauty. It looks like it's been woven from solidified mist, all flowing lines and impossible angles that catch the light like diamonds but move like smoke. As I step closer, drawn by something, I see patterns etched into its surface - the same marks from the door, from the daisies, from every dream I've ever had but couldn't remember upon waking.

The guys move with me, their presence steady at my back. The mist weaves between us, around us, through us, until I can't tell where it ends and we begin. Everything feels connected, like pieces of a puzzle finally shifting into place.

"Bree," Gray says softly, a world of meaning in that single syllable.

I reach for the crown, my fingers still shimmering with that strange light from the daisies. The mist surges, wrapping around my hand like a living thing, guiding me forward.

The moment my fingers brush the crown, a voice echoes through my mind - ancient and familiar all at once, like a memory of something that hasn't happened yet:

*"Welcome home, Queen of the Mist."*

The world goes white again, but this time I'm not afraid.

This time, I know I'm not alone.

# A Special Thank You

Dear Reader,

Thank you. From the bottom of my heart, thank you for stepping into the mist and joining Bree on this journey. Writing *Crown of the Mist* has been an emotional and deeply personal experience, and knowing that you took the time to read it means everything to me.

This book exists because of you—the readers who believe in stories of resilience, found family, and love that refuses to be denied. Whether you've been here from the beginning or are just discovering my work, I'm so incredibly grateful for your support.

If you enjoyed *Crown of the Mist*, the best way to help it reach more readers is by leaving a review. Your words matter more than you know, and they make a world of difference to indie authors like me. Even a short review helps others decide to take this journey, too.

This is just the beginning, and I can't wait to share more with you. Thank you again for your time, your support, and for believing in the magic of this story. I hope to see you in the next adventure.

With love and misty magic,

**Zora Stone**

# Sneak Peek: Into the Ether

# BREE

The white light doesn't fade—it shatters.

One moment I'm suspended in starlight, the ancient voice still echoing through my bones. The next, I'm stumbling backward as reality crashes in like a tidal wave. Sound rushes back in a disorienting flood: my ragged breathing, the creak of old floorboards, Theo's sharp intake of breath somewhere to my left.

My knees buckle.

Strong hands catch me before I hit the floor—Rhett's warmth at my right shoulder, Gray's steady grip on my left arm. My body should flinch like it always does when I'm touched without warning... but it doesn't. Not this time. Maybe I'm in shock. Or maybe something in me is finally too tired to resist.

"Easy," Rhett murmurs, his voice low and careful. "We've got you."

They guide me backward until the edge of the bed meets my legs, and I sink down gratefully, my whole body trembling with the aftershocks of whatever just happened.

I try to focus on the feel of his hand on my shoulder, Gray's fingers still wrapped around my forearm like he's afraid I might disappear. But everything feels strange, like I'm seeing the world through someone else's eyes. The mist that usually follows me everywhere has retreated, curling close to my skin like it's hiding.

Rhett's voice is low and careful. "Are you okay?"

Jace follows a second later, his worry barely masked by sarcasm. "What the hell was that?"

I open my mouth to say I'm fine—the automatic response I've perfected over years of deflection. But the words stick in my throat, caught between truth and habit.

"I..." I swallow hard, my hands shaking as I press them flat against my thighs. "I'm not fine."

The admission hangs in the air between us, heavier than any lie would have been. Wes moves closer, his dark eyes scanning my face with that quiet intensity that sees too much. Theo hovers near the foot of the bed, his analytical mind already working through what just happened.

"The crown," I whisper, staring down at my palms like they should still be holding something precious. The shimmer has faded now, but I can still feel the warmth, like a brand pressed into memory. The heat lingers. Like it left something inside me instead.

"You touched the crown," Theo says quietly, his voice carrying careful precision. "Whatever it was—it responded to you. And then everything collapsed."

"We all saw it," Gray adds, his sharp gaze never leaving my face.

I look toward where the impossible room had opened, where ancient stones had pulsed with their own inner light. But there's nothing there now. Just the same attic walls, the same dusty air. Even the crystalline daisies that had been growing through the floor are gone, leaving no trace they ever existed.

"The room," I say, confusion threading through my voice. "The space beyond the door—it was huge. Ancient. Where did it go?"

"Same place as the crown, I'm guessing," Jace mutters, running a hand through his hair. "Which is exactly nowhere we can follow."

Wes moves to the door, his footsteps silent on the old floorboards. He pulls it open cautiously, and I hold my breath, half-expecting that silver light to spill out again. Instead, there's just darkness. The faint outline of storage boxes and a broken light bulb hanging from a frayed cord.

"It's just a closet now," he says, his quiet voice carrying an edge of something I can't identify. "No crown. No glow." He runs his fingers along the doorframe, searching. "The symbol's gone too."

They all exchange looks—the kind of silent communication they've perfected over years of friendship. I should feel relieved that the mysterious door has returned to normal, that whatever magic pulled us here has faded back to ordinary wood and dust.

Instead, I feel empty. Like something vital has been carved out of my chest.

"Did anyone else hear..." I start, then stop. My voice feels too small. "Never mind."

"Hear what?" Rhett's voice is gentle but insistent.

"A voice." I wrap my arms around myself, suddenly cold. "When I touched the crown. It called me..." I swallow hard. "It called me queen."

Silence. Five sets of eyes watching me with expressions I can't quite read.

"We didn't hear anything," Theo says carefully. "Just the surge of power. The light."

Of course they didn't. Because whatever spoke to me wasn't meant for them.

It should be terrifying. It should feel like a mistake.

But it doesn't.

It feels like something from before. Before fear, before scars, before I started bracing for impact every time someone touched me.

Like the version of me that existed before everything got broken.

"This can't be real," I whisper, barely able to hear myself over the pounding in my chest. "Stuff like that doesn't just... happen."

No one argues with me. No one tries to explain.

I wrap my arms tighter around myself. "But I feel different."

The words taste strange. Too big. Too true.

"I don't know how. Just..." I exhale slowly. "Like something cracked open inside me. Not broken—just... not closed anymore."

The mist stirs at my words, unfurling from where it's been hiding against my skin. It doesn't reach for the others like it usually does—it stays close, protective, like it's guarding me from something.

"Hey," Rhett says softly, his thumb brushing over my shoulder. "Whatever just happened, we'll figure it out. Together."

"Will we?" The question slips out before I can stop it, raw and uncertain. I grip the blanket beneath me, grounding myself with something real. "Because right now I feel like I'm coming apart at the seams, and I don't even understand what's holding me together anymore."

Gray's hand tightens slightly on my arm, grounding me in the warmth of his touch. "You're not coming apart," he says softly. "But whatever this is..."

Theo steps forward, his voice calm and certain. "We've got you."

He meets my eyes, steady and unflinching.

"We see you, Bree."

I close my eyes, trying to make sense of the storm of sensation and memory swirling through me. The memory of the crown's weight in my hands, the voice that called me queen, the way the mist responded to my touch like it was coming home. None of it should be possible. Yet all of it feels more real than anything I've ever experienced.

"I keep waiting for this to feel wrong," I admit, opening my eyes to find them all watching me with expressions of fierce protectiveness and something deeper. Something I don't have words for.
"What just happened, what I felt... it should scare me. But it doesn't. It feels..."

"Right," Wes says from his spot by the door. "It feels right."

I nod, surprised by how much his understanding means. "How is that possible? How can something this impossible feel so natural?"

"Maybe," Jace says, his usual sardonic tone gentler than normal, "because it's not impossible. Maybe it's just been waiting for you to be ready for it."

The mist pulses once, like a heartbeat, and for a moment I swear I can feel the crown's presence even though it's gone. Like an echo of power that will never fully fade.

I stare at my hands again, flexing my fingers like I could still close around its weight. But there's only absence. The crown's disappearance feels like a phantom limb—something I should be able to reach for but can't quite touch.

It was real. I know it was real. The weight of it, the warmth, the way it seemed to sing when I touched it.

But now it's gone, and something inside me isn't. Something that feels ancient and new all at once, like a door that's been unlocked but not yet opened.

And something tells me it's not done with us yet.

*Continue the story in* **Into the Ether***, available now.*

# ABOUT THE AUTHOR

Zora Stone writes romantasy with teeth: fierce heroines, protective men who'd burn the world for them, and enough emotional wreckage to keep things interesting. When she's not plotting betrayals or steamy chaos, she's drinking iced coffee, dodging laundry, or daydreaming about enchanted forests.

You can find her online at:

Website: ZoraStone.com

TikTok | Instagram: @ZoraStoneAuthor

And on Amazon and Goodreads.

Want behind-the-scenes chaos and sneak peeks? ZoraStone.com/Influencers

# ALSO BY ZORA STONE

**The Ether Chronicles**

*Crown of the Mist*
*Into the Ether*
*Ashen Oath*
*Veil of Echoes*
*Shattering the Void*
*To the Final End*

**Arcanum Academy**

*Shadows of Change*
*Shadows Rising*
*Shadows Found*
*Shadows Revealed*